Small Town Dreams

Beginnings

Angela Tibbs

Small Town Dreams;

Beginnings

Bell Sheep Publishing

214 E 10th Street

Georgetown, Illinois 61846   USA

bellpublishing17@gmail.com

(217)474-0410

Editions ISBNS

Softcover; 979-8-9906561-0-9

E-book; 979-8-990651-1-6

Hardcover; 979-8-9906561-2-3

Table Of Contents

Introduction

I began to write small town dreams in nineteen ninety-seven when was a junior in high school. It started out originally for me as a way for to live a life that I always wanted to because in it I was all things I was my real life. By the time I had started at community college I had rewritten the novel at least four times.

As the years passed, characters came and went, and the story was rewritten and rewritten. Twenty- five years later I still hadn't got it written to where I felt that it was written well enough to be published. In the last two years I have written the small town dreams book series, and it has become the story I always thought the story would become.

As you read about the lives of Austin Reid and his cousin Lane, I hope that you find yourself within them and grow as they do. I hope that you experience the sadness, love, and joy within these pages that touch you in a way that you are never the same.

Chapter One
Beginnings

It was a stormy July fourth mornin in nineteen seventy- nine in Danville, Illinois. In the hospital a woman by the name of Ann Reid gave birth to her first child at eight o' clock that mornin, and named her daughter Lane Nichole Reid. Both Ann and her husband Paul were happy to have a little girl, but the doctor told them that their little girl was born with cleft lip and palate. Her parents acted quickly and took her to the St. Louis Children's Hospital. At three months old Lane went into surgery for the first time so they could close the openin in her lip, and the holes at the top of her mouth. After surgery the surgeon found a hole that they had missed, and she had to go back into surgery so they could close that one hole The doctors gave her splits to put on her arms so that she wouldn't touch where they operated. At five months Lane had her second surgery which the doctors made nasal corrections and worked on the upper gum. Three months later Lane had her third surgery where they worked on her upper palate.

Two years later, on January nineteenth in nineteen eighty
one Lee Ann Harper was born. Two days later Beverly Ann Schlatter
was born, and three days later Christine Helen Schlatter was born,
On April fifteenth I was born, David Ray Shackelford. On June sixth
Austin Andrew Reid was born, and the next day Eloise Dawn Killian
was born.

At the end of summer on August thirty first nineteen eighty-
three Lane's baby sister Harley Renee Reid was born. From the
beginnin it was clear that Lane and Harley were as different as night
and day. As a baby Harley was a force of nature and commanded the
room. Lane, on the other hand, was quiet and reserved just like a fly on
the wall. Lane was always so quiet that many times people didn't even
realize she was in the room.

In my own life, I was the youngest brother of three boys.
My two older brothers Asher and Aiden were always jealous of
me because I took up most of mama's attention. They would
always try to get me in trouble, and talk me into takin the blame
for them. My father would just laugh and think that it was funny,
and tell my mom that boys will be boys.

By the time all of us got to grade school Lee Ann, Beverly, Christine, and Eloise were just like sisters. Their mothers would have play dates for the four of them, so the girls were so close always showin off what they got their parents to buy them at the toy store. All four girls were very nice to me when I met them in school and helped me work through my shyness.

Up in Illinois grade school for Austin was good because he was popular with the girls even at a young age. For Lane, school was the place that she found out that she was different from everyone else. All the young kids made fun of her because she looked different from the rest of them. The kids didn't understand what was wrong with Lane, and many of them didn't want to because it was more fun to laugh at her. Lane, got to the point where she didn't want to even go to school because of the constant bullyin she had to endure.

Lane's third- grade year of school she had so many surgeries that she had to repeat her third-grade year again. That next year when havin to write young authors contest she took her book home even though the teacher told everyone they couldn't.. When the teacher found out that Lane had taken her book home, the teacher yelled at her in front of the entire classroom. Lane felt so very small, and felt that everyone in this world was goin to bullyin her because she deserved it.

The summer of nineteen eighty-nine Austin had just turned eight, and had also fallen in love with the girl across the street. Her name was Jessica Lynn Roth, and she was four years older than him. The Roth's had been Austin's family neighbor since before he was born. Austin and Jessica would spend the afternoon's after school ridin bikes, swimmin in the pool, playin basketball, and just enjoyin bein a kid.. Every evenin Austin and Jessica would watch the sunset either on Jessica's front porch or on Austin's front porch. If they watched the sunset on Austin's front porch he would walk her across the street to her front porch because it was dark, and Jessica was not the bravest person in the dark. It gave them an excuse to spend a few more minutes together before sayin good night.

Hope Barlett the next-door neighbor who was a year older than Austin had always liked him, but Austin had always liked Jessica. Hope was a short heavy-set girl with dark blue eyes and dark brown hair. Hope and her friend Eileen McClure would set on her porch swing, and the two would talk and watch Austin.

That Christmas Austin and Lane's uncle Thomas gave the two of them guitars as their present. Thomas had bought two new guitars, and their aunt Ruth told him that he had to either sell or give away two of them. Thomas decided to give the two guitars to his niece and nephew. The next January Austin and Lane started takin guitar lessons. Austin was doin great with the teacher his parents had signed him up to take lessons from. Lane took from the same teacher but was havin trouble understandin it. Lane's parents found a different teacher named Ernie Wolf, and he had been playin guitar himself since he was kid. Ernie had a different way of teachin, and Lane started to get it much quicker than before.

On a very cold snowy January Saturday afternoon Austin was in his room practin his guitar when the door opened and Jessica walked into the room. As she shut the door Jessica said, "You are gettin pretty good, Sunshine."

"Thank you." Austin said, as he looked up at her with his boyish grin as he played and started to sing the song "I Will Be There" by Dan Seals.

"I love that song because we made our own. Is this guitar goin to be the other woman in our relationship?"

"What do you mean?"

"You've never heard anyone say that before?" Jessica asked, as she sat down on the bed beside him.

"No." Austin replied, with his boyish grin as he put the guitar on the guitar stand by the bed.

"Are you goin to spend more time with that guitar than you do me?"

"You know I'll spend more time with you than this guitar."

"Good. Are we goin to watch your favorite movie anytime soon?" Jessica asked, with a big smile and a laugh.

Austin took her hand, and the two went downstairs to the livin room. An hour later Austin's mother walked into the livin room to check up on the two of them. She wasn't surprised to see Austin and Jessica settin close to each other on the couch, or that Jessica head on his shoulder as the two watched the Elvis movie "Live a little, Love a little."

6

After doin young authors in sixth grade, Lane became obsessed with writin stories. She would spend her time durin class writin instead of payin attention, and it's amazin she passed her classes that school year. One day while at school Lane got to thinkin about how all her friends in school seemed to be perfect in the way they looked and acted. Lane's thoughts then focused on how she didn't think she was born perfectly because of her cleft lip and palate. She then began to think that she would never live up to the friends she had in her life because to her they were perfect. They didn't have a deformity like she had, and seemed to get everything they wanted with little to no effort. As she picked up a pencil and a notebook she wrote these words;

I tried to be perfect in everyone's eyes

Inside I was torn apart

Great expectations were too much for me

I always seem to disappoint the people who

love me

Bein perfect is what one person can't be

Who's perfect, who's perfect, who's perfect

No one person can be perfect

Perfect, perfect, perfect, perfect

For years I've tried to live up to the

friends I chose

It had been a burden for me

Until the day I learned

The only person I had to please

was myself

Bein perfect is what one person can't be

Who's perfect, who's perfect, who perfect

No one person can be

perfect, perfect, perfect, perfect

Chapter Two

First Love

The summer of nineteen ninety- two the Americana television series premiered on television on Friday night at eight o' clock. Americana was based on an New York American family in the mid nineteen thirties. It was just as the New York Mafia was makin their mark in New York City as the five families were started to all work together.

It was no surprise that people all over the world were captivated by the show. Austin and Jessica would watch it every Friday with Austin's parents. At that time in his life Austin was learnin about Elvis Presley and the Memphis Mafia, and the show caught his interest because it was about the New York mob. Jessica started to get jealous because she thought that Austin only watched because of the actress Rosanna Aydelotte since they had watched every tv show she had done over the years.

Rosanna Aydelotte was a child actor, and the same age as Jessica. Rosanna had been on many television shows in her short life, and many were good ones but a few had flopped. Rosanna was a tall teenage girl with long blonde hair and piercin blue green eyes. Everyone liked her because she had the girl next door quality, but at the same time she brought the sense of vixen.

A stormy late July Saturday evenin Austin was in his room lyin on the bed just listenin to rain. All the sudden he got his notebook from his bookbag and started to write. Although he didn't know if he would even get answer to his letter Austin decided to write a letter to his favorite actress. After many times of tryin, and a bunch of paper around the trash can Austin finally got the letter to where he was happy with it. It read;

Dear Rosanna,

My name is Austin Reid, and I am a huge fan of Americana. I watch it every Friday night at eight o' clock. I have watched all of the television shows you have been in. Will you please send me a signed picture back I would appreciate it a lot.

Your biggest fan,

Austin Reid

After Austin got the letter ready to mail, he held it in his hands, closed his eyes, and said, "Dear lord, I ask that this letter gets to Rosanna Aydelotte, and she reads it. I ask that you make a way for us to be friends and in the future we could do some projects together in movies or tele- vision. I don't know what I'm here on earth to do, but I ask that you would help me find my path I'm suppose to walk. I ask this in Jesus name amen and amen."

Three weeks later the Georgetown Fair had come to town for the year. The second night of the fair was the talent show, and Austin was in it and he sang "Moon Over Georgia." It was Austin and Jessica favorite song, and it reminded Jessica of her favorite movie "Gone With The Wind." With each performance Austin was startin to get a small fanbase with people around the local communities. Jessica was happy when his fans came up to him to say hello or want to take a picture with him. Although Jessica was gettin a little jealous because they were takin the time he had to spend with her away.

After the talent show was over Austin was playin skee ball while Jessica was ridin rides with her friends. He had just finished a game when Hope walked up beside him and asked, "Do you want play a game with a bet?"

"What kind of a bet?" Austin asked, with his boyish grin.

"If I win, I get to give you a kiss."

"And if I win?"

"You can give me a kiss, or I can buy you somethin from your favorite food stand."

No less than five feet away Jessica and her friends were watchin
the interaction between Ausitn and Hope. Jessica's friends could
tell by the look on Jessica's face that she was very upset. Her
friends knew that there would be a fight between Jessica and Hope
over Austin sooner rather than later.

"Ok, are you ready to play." Austin said, crackin his boyish smile
as he put his quarters into the slots.

Hope put their quarters in the slots and skee balls came down,
and the two started to play the game. Hope was in the lead by twenty points
at the start, but right at the end Austin came back with two fifty points shots
and won. Jessica smiled from ear to ear when she saw that Austin had won.
Hope bought Austin and an elephant ear so disappointed that he didn't give
her a kiss.

Austin and Jessica were ridin on the ferris wheel around ten o' clock.
When it stopped at the top as the wind blew Jessica's hair, she looked at
him and asked, "Would you have kissed her?"

"You saw that?" Austin asked, a little surprised with a laugh.

"Yes, I did.."

"I would have had to do it because it was bet."

"Because she won you would've kissed her?" Jessica asked, raisin her voice gettin upset.

"Yes, I would have because it was a bet." Austin replied, seein her blue green eyes filled with fire. "But, I would have never kissed her the way I kiss you."

Hope, Reese, Peyton, Maddie, Eileen, and a few other friends were walkin down the midway and heard the fight between Austin and Jessica. Hope just smiled because although she didn't get to kiss him she had caused a problem between them. Elieen and the other girls just shook their heads and laughed because of the big smile on Hope's face so proud of herself.

"Austin Reid, I can't believe you would say that to me." Jessica said, very upset with Austin's answers.

"Satnin, chill out." Austin said, as he put his hand in hers. "Just be thankful that I won, and you didn't have to see me kiss her."

"Really? You know I would have had to beat both of you up if you had kissed her."

Austin cracked his boyish grin as he leaned in and gave her a kiss just as the ferris wheel started to start goin around again. Deep down

Jessica knew that Austin was tellin the truth because if he wanted to kiss her he would have.

The followin hot August Monday mornin the nineteen ninety two-nineteen ninety- three school year started. Austin joined Lane in the junior high while Jessica was a freshman in high school. Jessica was a little anxious because he was in the same school as Hope, and she believed that Hope would take advantage of it.

On a chilly early September mornin, Austin was waitin for the bus when he heard a voice say, "You're waitin for the bus kind of early."

"I know." Austin replied, crackin his boyish smile.

"Austin, can I kiss you?"

"That's not a good idea."

"Are you scared that you might like it?"

"Jessica may walk up any minute."

"So you are scared you might like it."

"No, I'm not scared." Austin said, flashin his boyish smile thinkin he should just get it over with.

Hope quickly kissed Austin on the lips, and the two were still kissin when Jessica walked up to the bus stop and saw them. She stood there very quietly for a few minutes not believin what she was seein. After takin a deep breath she said, "Excuse me, Hope what the hell do you think you're doin?"

"I'm gettin the kiss I didn't get at the fair." Hope replied, as she quit kissin Austin and smiled.

"Austin?"

"She kissed me before I could push her away." Austin explained, tellin the truth.

The bus drove up a few minutes later Austin, Jessica, Hope, and a few other kids got on the bus to ride to school. Austin had to ride the bus alone that day in his seat because Jessica set with some of her friends. The next two weeks were hard for Austin because Jessica wasn't talkin to him at all, and Hope was talkin to him anytime she got the chance. By the time the fourteen days were over Austin and Jessica would ride the bus settin so far apart, but as they looked at each other with their eyes they said so much.

On a rainy September Tuesday evenin Austin walked over to Jessica's house in the rain. He wasn't at all surprised to see her sittin on the porch

15

swing watchin the storm rollin through. As he made is way up onto the porch Austin said, "That rain is cold."

"You look like a drenched rat." Jessica said, laughin with a big smile on her face.

"Thank you, are you goin to talk to me now?"

As the lightin flashed and the thunder rolled Austin made his way over to the porch swing where Jessica was sittin. When he got ready to set down Jessica asked, "Yes, but why did you kiss Hope?"

"I didn't kiss her." Austin said, as he sat down on the porch swing. "She kissed me."

"When I walked up the two of you were kissin each other pretty good."

"Maybe I just wanted to get it over with so that she would leave me alone."

"Do you really think she's goin to leave you alone now?" Jessica asked, as she got the blanket that was on the back of the porch swing.

"No, I didn't think about that."

"I knew that she would take advantage of you bein in the same school with her."

"Just relax." Austin said, as he helped her put the blanket around them. "You know you have nothin to worry about."

"After what happened at the bus stop I'm not sure." Jessica said, with a very serious look on her face.

The two talked for a few minutes before they snuggled together and watched the thunderstorm roll through. Across the street Hope was settin on her porch swing also watched the storm, but when she saw Austin and Jessica snuggled up together on the porch swing she wasn't very happy. She had thought for sure that she had broken them up when they hadn't talked for two weeks.

As the November chill came Austin and Lane's grandpa Reid quickly went downhill and passed away on November twenty second, and Lane would remember it always because it was the same day that President Kennedy was shot and killed. The entire Reid family took his passin very hard, and there was a large void in all of their lives. The evenin of the visitation Jessica was by Austin's side, and when Hope's family arrived you could feel the tension in

17

the air. Once her family went through the line Hope made her way over to where Austin was standin, and as she gave him a hug she said, "Austin, I'm so sorry. You know that I'm here for you if you need me."

"Thank you." Austin said, as he hugged her with tears fallin down his eyes.

"Your grandpa was a good man and he will be missed."

Jessica let Hope hug him for a few minutes as she stood beside him, and then once she thought it was enough time Jessica said, "Hope, you need to step back from Austin now."

"It's his grandpa's visitation, and I was just givin him a hug. Chill out, Jessi." Hope said, as she broke the hug from Austin.

"You need to walk away right now."

"Austin's my friend and I'm not just goin to walk away because you tell me to." Hope said, with a very serious look in her eyes.

Seein that there was goin to be a huge scene Eileen walked up to Hope and said, "Hope, let's go visit with Reese and Peyton, and you can talk to Austin later."

Hope walked away from Austin, and went over to where Peyton and Reese were standin. Even though she was talkin to them every once in a while she and Austin would make eye contact. Austin was talkin to other family members and friends hearin stories of his grandpa. Austin didn't realize it but Jessica would catch him lookin over at Hope, and by the expression on her you could tell she was very upset.

November twenty seventh was the day of Grandpa Reid's funeral, and it would be a day that Austin, Lane, and the rest of the grand-children would never forget. That evenin Jessica's parents had a small gatherin for friends and family for Jessica's birthday. An hour into the party many weren't surprised that Austin and Jessica had slipped off by themselves because they been around so many people all day.

Austin and Jessica were lyin on her bed lookin up at the cut out stars glowin on the cecilin when Jessica said, "I know this day will be sad from now since Grandpa Reid was buried today."

"It will be." Austin said, as he looked over at her with sadness in his eyes. "But celebratin your birthday will also make it happy for me."

"Are you sure? I hate that my birthday will make you sad now."

"I'm sure." Austin said, as he pulled a little black box out of his dress pants. "I do have a present for you. Do you want it?"

"Yes." Jessica said, as she set up on her side and set her head on her hand.

"Are you sure?"

"Reid, give it to me."

"You really want it?" Austin asked, as he moved it to where she couldn't get it.

"Austin Reid, let me have it." Jessica said, as she tried to get the box from him.

Austin finally handed her the black box and Jessica opened it findin a heart shaped locket. She opened the heart and found a recent picture of them. When she looked at the right side, there was a picture of them when they were very young. Jessica started to cry and as she wiped her eyes she said, "Thank you, I love it."

"That way we can change the picture on the left as we grow older." Austin said, crackin a big grin. "But we can always see how young we were when we fell in love."

"I love you, Sunshine." Jessica said, as she gave him a kiss on the lips.

Austin and Jessica had just started kissin when the door
opened and Jessica's sister Mia said, "Jessi, Austin, everyone
is wonderin where you are."

"Ok, we're comin." Jessica said, crackin a smile as she looked at
her sister.

"If mom or dad would have caught you two." Mia said, with a smile
and a laugh.

"We are only kissin, Mia." Austin said, with his boyish grin. "It's not
like were takin any farther."

"You are eleven years old, Austin Reid. I don't want to hear that
kind of talk from you."

"Why Mia? You don't like seein us do the same thing you are doin
With your boyfriend?"

"I don't want to hear this." Mia said, as she started to shut the
door. "You two are too young to even think about it."

Austin and Jessica just laughed as Mia shut the door. After
stealin a few more kisses from each other. The two then made their
way to the livin roo, with everyone else.

Within a matter of weeks it was Christmas Eve, Jessica walked over to Austin's house around two o' clock that afternoon because she couldn't wait to give Austin's present. After sayin hello to the rest of his family, Jessica made her way upstairs to Austin's room where she found him settin on the bed lookin through a scrapbook puttin pictures in it. As she sat on the bed beside him she asked, "What are you doin with that?"

"I decided to put pictures of us from this year's fair in it." Austin replied, as he looked up at her with a grin.

"I can't believe that we decided to start that two years ago." Jessica said, with a big smile. "But there is one thing we haven't done yet."

"What's that?"

"We need to write our weddin vows to each other, so that we have a record of it for when we get married."

"I'm goin to have to think about that for a while."

"That's ok." Jessica said, crackin a big smile. "I better think about what I'm goin to write to. How about we write them in there on Valentine's Day."

"Ok." Austin said, as he got somethin from under his pillow, and handed it to her. "Merry Christmas."

Jessica unwrapped the present and was surprised it was a copy of gone with the wind book. It was the book that she wanted to read, but her parents never bought it for her because they thought it was too graphic because it caused such a stir when it was published in nineteen thirty-six.

"Thank you." Jessica said, with a smile from ear to ear. "I'll have to hide this from my parents so they don't see it."

"Yes, you will." Austin said, with a laugh. "Although, I'm sure you will be readin it soon because you always have you nose in a book, or watchin the movie "Gone with the Wind" the movie again."

"I can't help that I like the movie."

"I know."

"The present I got for you is for both of us." Jessica said, as she took a small black box out of her pocket.

"What did you do?" Austin asked, crackin his boyish smile.

"I got us promise rings."

"Promise rings?"

"We're promisin each other right now that we will marry each other one day."

"But, one day we are goin to get married." Austin said, with the funniest look on his face.

Takin Austin's ring out of the box Jessica placed the ring on his right hand and said, "I know, Austin. Accept this ring with the promise that I'm ready to be yours and yours alone."

Austin took the other ring out of the box, and as he placed the ring on Jessica's right ring finger he said, "Accept this ring with the promise that I'm ready to be yours and your alone."

A few days later Austin spent New Year's Eve with Jessica and her family. The two kissed at midnight makin sure that they would be together for another year. Austin also spent the night at the Roth house, but he had to sleep on the couch. No surprise the next mornin when Jessica's mother got up and walked into the livin room she saw Jessica and Austin sleepin on the couch bed together. As she stood there and looked at the two of them, she knew that Austin would be her son-in-law one day.

The new year started and Lane had surgery in January. She missed six weeks of school. She enjoyed not goin to school, and gettin to watch tv every day. Lane also was happy she didn't hear people makin fun of her all day long.

In Saltillo Eloise and I started datin, but she was more focused on
her dancin. She wanted to go to Julliard in New York City when she
grew up. Lee Ann, Beverly, Christine, and Eloise all took dance
class from the same dance teacher in Tupelo. It was another aspect
of the friendship they shared, but the other girls just danced for fun.
Beverly and Christine wanted to bring the singin group the Schlatter
quartet back, but only it was goin to be called The Schlatter's. Back
in the early thirties to the late eighties the Schlatter quartet was very
big in Mississippi, and all around the united state Somethin had happened in the eighties that made the family end the musical legacy of the
Schlatter quartet. Beverly and Christine asked everyone in their family about
it, but no one would tell them. They had even asked around the small town
of Saltillo, but the towns people would tell them they needed to ask their
family. It didn't matter though Beverly and Christine were both determined
young girls who were goin to make the new legacy of the Schlatter's be better
than in the past. Christine's parents were very surprised when she asked if
she could learn to play drums. They thought that she would want to play
keyboard or guitar, but the drums was somethin out of left field. Beverly
started takin guitar lessons from their grandpa Hugo Schlatter. He was an
original member of the Schlatter quartet, and when Beverly would ask him to

tell her about the group. Hugo Schlatter would tell his granddaughter that he just didn't want to talk about it. No surprise at all that Lee Ann started takin bass guitar lessons from Beverly's great uncle, and Eloise started takin piano lessons from Beverly's grandma Darlene.

Back in Illinois Austin got a letter in the mail, and he was so excited because he knew who it was from. Austin ran up to his room and opened the letter bein so excited at what he received. It was a signed autograph picture of Rosanna Aydelotte and a standard letter thankin him for bein her fan. Just as Austin got done puttin the signed eight by ten picture in a picture frame, Jessica walked into the doorway and said, "What are you doin, Sunshine?"

"Puttin my new picture in a frame." Austin replied, with a big grin that looked like the cat that got the canary.

"What new picture?"

"My autographed picture of Rosanna Aydelotte."

"You wrote a fan letter to her?"

"Yes, I did."

"Why did you do that?" Jessica asked, as she sat down on the bed beside him.

"I'm a huge fan of hers, and it's not hurtin anything for me to send a fan letter to her."

"I know that, guess I'm a little bit jealous."

"You jealous? When you know that I will probably never meet her."

"That's true, but what if you ever do meet her?"

"You'll be right beside him holdin my hand." Austin said, with a smile as he looked into her blue green eyes.

Across town Lane was takin a nap, and in her dream she was standin on the Georgetown Fair stage goin over the song list for the concert that night at the fair. She was practicin a new song and couldn't get It right. A tall muscular man with greyin dark brown hair asked, "Honey, what's wrong?"

"I can't get the song right," Lane replied, gettin very upset.

"Hey, guys can you start it again, please."

The band started playin Lane started singin the song, and when she got to the second verse she stumbled again. The man watchin her walked up to the stage, jumped on the stage, grabbed his guitar, and they tried the song one more time.

After gettin through the song list Lane went on the bus to relax. She had just closed her eyes closed when the tall muscular man walked in, set down, and said, "Baby, is everything all right?"

"I don't want to mess this up," Lane replied, as she looked into his dark brown eyes. "I've dreamed of playin on this stage since I was a kid."

"You'll do great."

"J. B. How do you know?"

As he moved a piece of hair from her face J.B. said, "Because you've worked for this all your life, and God will let you shine tonight."

"You think so?"

"Baby, I know so." J.B. said, as he leaned down and given her a kiss.

Two hours later it was time for the concert to start. The openin act was on the stage, and Lane had got her stage clothes on. Lane was lookin at herself in the mirror when J.B. walked into the bedroom and put his arms around her. As he kissed her on the neck he said, "You are gonna do great, baby. And I'll be right beside you playin my guitar."

With a big smile she put her hand on his and said, "Thank you for believin in me."

"I always will believe you, Lane." J.B. said, as he looked at her through the mirror.

"How did I get so lucky to find a man as great as you?"

"You asked god for man, and he blessed you with me."

Lane giggled and smiled as she looked at him before the two shared a few kisses. J.B. and Lane then set down on the couch. The two bowed their heads as Lane began to pray. She said, "Dear lord, I want your light to shine bright in me today. Please touch someone in the crowd with the lyrics to the songs you have written through me. Let the light shine bright through the entire band too. Everyone shines tonight for your glory, amen and amen."

Lane heard the announcer say, "Ladies and gentlemen, Lane Reid and the Inner Circle."

Sunday mornin Austin and his family walked into church, Hope, Eileen, Maddy, Reese, and Peyton watched Austin walked right over to where Jessica was standin. Austin and Jessica then walked into the sanctuary and set down in their seats in the pew. Church started on time that mornin, and after the choir sung mornin hymn the preacher stepped up to the podium and said, "Please turn to in your bibles to Matthew 13;47. When you find it say amen."

Randomly people in the congregation began to say amen. After a handful of people said amen, the preacher began to preach his message.

"Jesus is teachin here. Every fisherman back in those days used a net to catch fish. Once it is full it's pulled into the boat and is gone through to discern the good and the bad."

"Preach it!" An older gentleman yelled, sittin in the back row.

"When Jesus comes back he's bringin up a large net filled with all sorts of people. His angels are goin to go through them, and the good will be separated from the bad at the end of the age. The wicked will be thrown into the fiery furnace of fire where there will be whallin and the gnashin of teeth." The preacher said, lookin into his bible.

"Amen!"

"Which fish are you? A good fish or a bad fish, and where will you spend the rest of your life?"

"Oh, come on!"

"In this life we shouldn't have to worry about the angels thrownin us in the fiery furnace, but we should live our live praisin the lord. We shouldn't want to be a charcoal briquette."

The congregation laughed after a few seconds gettin what the pastor was tryin to convey. A few people in the congregation began to look over at other people in the congregation who they thought might be charcoal briquettes because of the way they lived.

"Preach it!"

"Let's have it."

"In our lives we all have choices to make we can be told about the lord and why he saved us until we're blue in the face. The choice is up to us if we want to make him our lord and savior. We have to let people see how fun it is to be saved from the world of darkness. "

"Preach it."

"Let's bow our heads, dear lord, thank you for your word this mornin. I just ask that you bring it back to our remembrance this next week, I also ask that angels be with them as they go to the high-ways and byways on this earth. Let them be a light in someone else's darkness. I ask this in Jesus name, amen and amen."

The congregation said amen in agreement, and the endin hymns were sung. The quietness was broken with chatter as people began to catch up with the local gossip.

The end of the school year came quickly that year, Austin and Jessica spent every day together since Mia babysit his younger brother and sister. It was no surprise that Hope was watchin Austin and Jessica all summer long jealous of Jessica because she had the boy that Hope wanted.

On a Thursday afternoon Austin and Jessica were swimmin in the pool with their siblins. Hope watched from her back porch, and daydreamed that it was her spendin time with Austin instead of Jessica. She didn't even notice when Austin and Jessica went into the house for a break.

Inside the house Austin and Jessica had dried off, and had went upstairs to Austin's room to spend some time by themselves. As they were lyin on the bed together lookin up at the cecilin Jessica said, "I can't believe that we actually got away from my sister."

"Well, I'm sure Brandon, Sophia, and Caleb are keepin her busy." Austin said, with a laugh as he set up and looked into her blue eyes.

"I bet they are."

Austin just smiled as he leaned down and gave her a kiss. Jessica soon put her arms around his neck as the moment got intense between the two of them. Austin and Jessica did want people in love do, and the fact that they were teenagers didn't matter. Just as the passion between them began to boil over Jessica said, "Austin, stop. You and I are both not ready for that."

"How come you think we're not ready?" Austin said, as he looked into her blue eyes confused.

"We're just not." Jessica said, as she pushed him back with her hands. "Besides, we have the rest of our lives to do that when we're old enough."

"Ok. I think you listen too much in church."

"Reid, don't do that to me." Jessica said, as she looked at him with a funny expression. "I know you listen in church too, and it will not hurt us to wait a little longer. Besides, I don't think that we should do somethin just because everyone else is doin it."

"You do have a point." Austin replied, disappointed. "If the pastor only knew the kids in his congregation that have crossed the line, but set there in church just smiling listenin to him talk."

That summer Jessica's parents decided to give her the nineteen sixty- five Ford mustang that her grandfather had owned. It was a little rough around the edges, so Jessica had to help her father fix it up. Austin was amazed when he walked over to her house, and saw her workin on the car. It was no surprise that Austin was soon learnin how to work on the car too. That summer did pass very quickly and before they knew it the Georgetown Fair had come into town.

On Tuesday evenin Austin and Jessica were in the Georgetown Fair talent show. Jessica's parents were very surprised that Austin talked Jessica into singin with him on stage. Many of their classmates heard the two of them were singin and they had to go to cheer them on. Standin backstage Austin and Jessica were waitin for their names to be called, and Austin could tell that Jessica was terrified.

"Satnin, are you ok?" Austin asked, lookin into her terrified eyes.

"I don't think I can do this." Jessica replied, as she looked at him terrified.

"Yes, you can. I'm goin to be right there on stage beside you."

"No, I can't do this.."

"Satnin, it's ok. I'll go on stage by myself."

"Sunshine, I'm sorry. I thought I could do this."

"It's ok, Satnin." Austin replied, as he kissed her on the forehead.

"Thank you." Jessica said, as she took a sigh of relief. "I really thought I would be able to sing with you on stage tonight, but my nerves aren't goin to let me."

Austin and Jessica's names were called, but only Austin walked out on the stage with his guitar in his hand. He put the guitar around his neck and made sure it was in tune. As the crowd set on the edge of their seats, Austin started to sing the song "Love Me." After he sang the chorus and verse, he was gettin ready to start singin the next verse when Jessica walked out on stage singin the song "Don't." Austin looked back at her surprised, and he just cracked his boyish smile as he strummed his guitar. Then Austin and Jessica made the songs fit together so well that the entire crowd was amazed. Austin and Jessica's parents looked at each other with both shock and surprise because they didn't know their children could sing that good together. In the crowd there was a girl named Jaelyn Somerled, she was a tall skinny girl with shinin green eyes a bubbly spirit, and she had a crush on Austin. Jaelyn was like Jessica she could always find a reason to smile. Jaelyn was in the same grade as Harley and was two years younger than Austin. Since Jaelyn was one of Harley's closest friends she had spent time at Austin's house when Harley and her friends would go over for a sleep over that Sophia was havin. Jaelyn had also told her older sister Jaedyn that she was goin to be Austin's girlfriend and marry him one day. Jaedyn told Jaelyn that she was crazy because Austin was so in love with Jessica he would never even notice her.

After the talent show was over that evenin Austin and Jessica were in the food building eatin curly fries and drinkin orange shake ups. Austin's cousin Harley walked up with a group of friends and said, "Jaelyn would like to take a picture with you. She's one of your biggest fans."

"Ok." Austin said, as he finished eatin his fry and took a drink of his shake up.

Austin got up and walked over to where Jaelyn was standin, and Harley took a few pictures. Settin at the table Jessica was a little upset because she didn't want to share Austin with anyone especially with his fans. She braced a smile as Austin looked at her with a big smile enjoyin the attention he was gettin from his fans.

As Harley took the last picture Jaelyn looked up at Austin and said, "Thank you, for takin pictures with me."

"You're welcome, Jaelyn." Austin replied, with a big smile as he looked into her bright green eyes. "I will always make time for my friends."

"I'm your friend?" Jaelyn said, as she looked up into his ice blue eyes.

"Yes, you are...You're at my house all the time with my cousin and her friends, and we've gotten to know each other."

Jaelyn just smiled at him so big, and her green eyes were glowin so bright. As she looked into his eyes she wondered if she would be in his future as more than a friend. In that moment, Austin and Jaelyn saw a spark in each other's eyes that they neither one could forget.

The followin Monday the nineteen ninety-three nineteen ninety four school year started and Jessica still didn't like that Austin and Hope would still be in the junior high school together. Jessica was a sophomore in high school. For Lane eighth grade year was goin to go as slow as the other years had, but she had her writin to look forward to. She loved to go off into a different world durin class where life wasn't as hard, and she could be the person she wanted to be. That person who was popular, talented, and not bein bullied because of the way that she looked.

On a rainy August day around eleven thirty, Austin was sittin at the back next to the wall all by himself. Hope set down beside him and with a smile said, "How's your day, Austin?"

"Bornin as usual." Austin said, as he took a bite of A chip. "And how is yours?"

"Better now, Mr. Reid."

"Cute."

"I thought so."

"You just don't give up do you?"

"Not when it's somethin that I want." Hope said, crackin a big smile as she looked at him.

"Well, as long as I'm with Jessica you are never goin to have me." Austin said, with a very serious look on his face.

"We'll see." Hope said, as she cracked a big smile as she thought of all the ways that she could steal him away from Jessica.

August quickly turned into September, and there was a different chill in the Illinois air than there had ever been before. There was a sense of somethin was goin to happen, but nobody really knew what that was goin to be. It scared them a little bit because the chill seemed to be much colder than in had been in years past. For the teenagers in the small town, it was just another autumn that they had to be in school.

Austin and Jessica were sittin on Austin front porch as the sun went down on a chilly Friday evenin. Austin and Jessica were snuggled together under a blanket watchin the sunset. With a big smile Jessica said, "I can't believe two more years, and I'll be out of high school."

"I know." Austin said, with a disappointed look on his face. "Then I'll have four years of school without you here with me."

"You know that I'll come back to visit. You know I want to be a fighter pilot."

"I know." Austin replied, as he looked at her. "And you are goin to be one bad ass woman too."

"You think so?" Jessica said, with a laugh.

"I know so, and one thing I do love about you is that you're scared of the dark."

"Why do you love that about me?"

"Because I get to walk you home after the sun goes down."

"Well, I do like that part too." Jessica said, with a big grin. "I love that I get so spend some more time with you."

The two set on swing for quite a while after the sun set before Austin walked Jessica home. No surprise, Jessica's mother was standin in the front door lookin for her to walk up the driveway. Austin walked her up to the door, gave her a kiss goodnight, and then made his way back to his house.

September twentieth was like any other day. Austin, Jessica, and Hope got on the school bus at their normal time. After school was out for the day, the bus ride home was so different. Jessica Hope, and a few other girls she set by on the bus were havin a blast talkin about boys and other things that girls that age talked about.

At three thirty that afternoon Jessica decided to go for a bike ride. She asked her dad if she could go for a bike ride as he worked on his car. As she rode out of the driveway, her father heard a car rev its engine but didn't think anything of it. As Jessica walked her bike, her sister Mia drove down the road runnin an errand in town and the two smiled and waved at each other. Twenty minutes later when Mia came back down the road to towards the house she noticed that Jessica's bike was on the side of the road, but Jessica was nowhere to be found. Mia drove home to tell her dad what she had found. Mia's father called his wife, and his wife called the police. Soon people from Georgetown came out to help look for Jessica. When Austin and his family got home at four fifteen, Mia ran over and the family what had happened. Austin's family quickly joined the rest of the people in town who were searchin for Jessica. Jessica wasn't found the next two days, and her mother knew on the third day that Jessica wasn't goin to come home because someone had took her on purpose.

The days started to pass which turned into weeks, and soon it was a month. The police were lookin for Jessica still, but there had been no updates about her whereabouts. Jessica family was distraught, and Austin had shut down completely because they hadn't found Jessica. Austin was stayin in his room after he got home at night from his grandma's house, and his guitar was settin in his stand not bein played at all because he had dropped out of lessons. Not only were Austin's parents gettin worried, but Jessica's parents were also worried about him. One night his parents had gone out and his aunt came to babysit him and his siblins, and Austin found the key to the liquor cabinet that was in the dinin room. When his aunt wasn't lookin Austin took his first bottle of whiskey out of the cabinet.

Austin went to church every Sunday with his parents always dressin in a three-piece suit. Austin had always liked dressin in a suit because he said it made him look good. After church one Sunday they had a potluck dinner for Jessica's family, and Austin was sittin at a table all by himself watchin everyone else talk and laugh. Austin had the most heartbreakin look on his face as he took a drink of soda pop when Jaelyn set down next to him and said, "Austin, how are you doin?"

"I'm all right, I guess." Austin replied, as he looked over at her wonderin what she wanted. "What are you up to? Why aren't you playin tag with the rest of your friends?"

"You looked like you needed a friend, so I wanted to come over and say hi."

"I looked that bad, huh?"

"You look like you need to someone to talk to." Jaelyn said, as she looked into his sad ice blue eyes. "Why don't you talk to me."

"You're too young. You wouldn't understand."

"Reidsy, I'm only two years younger than you. I'm not too young to know what you have to say because I lost my grandpa not too long ago, and I know what loss feels like."

"Ok." Austin said, crackin his boyish grin. "Jaelyn, you are such a sweet girl. I'm glad to have you as my friend."

"I know this time is hard for you." Jaelyn said, seein the pain in Austin's eyes. "But please talk to me even if you just have to vent."

"Ok, sweetness."

"Sweetness, what is that?"

"Your nickname." Austin replied, crackin his boyish smile. "I always give nicknames to those people who become special to me."

"You do? I don't want to make you sad again, but what is Jessica's nickname?"

"Jessica's nickname is satnin."

"Why do you call her that?" Jaelyn asked, just wantin to know.

"I'm a big Elvis fan."

"Yes, everyone knows that."

"Elvis called his mother Gladys and his wife Priscilla that name because they were very special to him." Austin explained, with a very serious look on his face. "Since Jessica was that special to me I started callin her by that name."

"Will you call any other girl that comes into your life now that name?"

"No, that name I will not use again because it's Jessica's."

"That's kinda what I figured."

"Sweetness, do you want to take a walk outside away from all these people where we can talk alone?"

"Yes, cupcake."

"Why did you call me cupcake?" Austin asked, as he started to get out of the chair.

"It's my new nickname for you, so I won't call you Reidsy like everyone else in town." Jaelyn said, as she got up out of the chair.

Ten few feet away Hope, Maddy, Peyton, Reese, Eileen, Jaedyn, and a few other girls were sittin at a table talkin when they noticed Austin and Jaelyn gettin up from their table and start to head out of the room. Hope was wonderin if he would ever give her a real chance to be with him. Although she hadn't made it known to anyone Reese Demski also liked Austin. The two got to know each other when Austin ran track his sixth-grade year. Breakin the silence of what usually was a very loud group Jaedyn said,

"I wonder where the two of them are goin?"

"Well, she's bolder than anyone of us" Peyton said, with a laugh knowin few of them wanted to talk to him.

"I wouldn't know what to say to him." Reese said, as she took a drink of her tea.

"I wouldn't either.." Hope said, makin up an excuse.

"I'm sure he's goin out of his mind wonderin where Jessica is at." Maddy said, sayin what no one else dared to say.

"The only question is.." Eileen said, as she looked at all of them. "Is what will happen to him when she's found."

Everyone looked at Elieen knowin she was right because no one knew if Jessica was goin to be found alive. Everyone had hope that she would be found alive and would come home safe and sound. Still, it had been four weeks and she hadn't been found yet.

As the October days seemed to pass by very slowly, Austin started spendin a lot of time with Jaelyn. His mother would take him to her house, or she would come over to his house. Many Sundays she would have lunch with the Reid family, and she would visit with Austin for a few hours before her mother would pick her up. On occasion Austin would go over and have lunch with her family and visit before one of his parents picked him up. All the girls in town knew that Jaelyn was the one who was keepin Austin sane durin this dark time. Many of the girls were jealous of her because she was two years younger than Austin, and wasn't even in the same school as him.

When the month of November started on that Monday mornin, Austin could feel a familiar chill in the air, and as the wind blew he believed that he could feel Jessica's presence around him. Austin didn't know what it meant or what was goin on, but all he knew was that she was around him. On that very cold November Monday evenin, Austin had played the last song he played for Jessica which was "Always Have, Always Will." It was the song he was learnin in guitar lessons at the time she disappeared. Austin picked up the picture he had of the two of them on the nightstand and kissed her before puttin it back on the nightstand. He crawled into bed, got comfortable, and fell asleep quickly.. When he first drifted off to dreamland he started dreamin about Jaelyn and how thankful she was there for him. Makin him smile and laugh durin the roughest time in his life. When he turned over, Austin saw Jessica settin on the edge of the bed next to him. After takin a moment to gather himself he asked, "Jessica, where are you? What happened to you?"

As Jessica put her hand on his hand shewith sadness in her eyes, she said, "Someone murdered me six weeks ago for his own pleasure."

"No, that can't be true. You're comin back to me." Austin said, with tears runnin down from his eyes.

"Austin, you will have to learn to live without me."

"But what if I don't want to?"

"You have to." Jessica said, as she ran her fingers through his hair.

"Why?" Austin asked, as tears ran now his face.

"Because that's the way it supposed to be. You are supposed to walk the path of life you were sent down to earth to do."

"Without you life isn't worth livin."

"Sunshine, it will be all right."

"How can you say that? You are not here to walk beside me, and the life we dreamed of with never happen." Austin said, as a flood of tears fell from his eyes.

"Reid, it will be all right because God has a good plan for you." Jessica said, as she ran her fingers through his hair. "And you never know.."

"You never know what?" Austin said, very confused as he looked at her.

"Sunshine, you never know when you least expect it I will come back into your life and stay forever." Jessica said, with a big smile and laugh.

Austin woke up in a cold sweat and looked around the room lookin for Jessca before he laid his head back down on the pillow. The hardest part for Austin was knowin that he had to move on with his life without her. He spent the rest of the night cryin in his pillow loud enough that his little brother Brandon could hear him.

The next mornin Austin went to school, and he was very quiet all day. His friends in the school tried to get him to join in the childlike games that they were playin but he just kept to himself. Jaedyn could tell that somethin was botherin him, and so to keep the other kids away from him she was around him all day. Austin didn't open up to her, but he was thankful that she was there for him. That evenin on the six o'clock news a report came across that a body had been found across the border in Indiana. The reporters didn't have the name of the who it was yet, and then just gave need to know information that they had collected. As Austin watched the report he knew that it was Jessica, and he knew that he would never see her again. Austin ran upstairs and locked himself in his room cryin for the next few hours. A part of Austin died that day because the innocence he had in his life had left because of someone's selfish needs.

The days started to pass very slow as the investigation into who the teenager was started. After weeks of not knowin, everyone heard the news they didn't want to hear, and the teenager found in the cornfield was Jessica Roth. The only questioned remain was who could do such a bad thing to an innocent teenage girl. Three weeks later Jessica's family finally got to have her funeral. Many people attended the visitation mournin the loss of the sweet teenage girl they knew and loved. Austin took the day of the funeral very hard because he was sayin goodbye to someone he really loved. That day Austin asked Jessica's mother if he could have the the locket and ring that she wore every day. Jessica's mother told him that when they found her she wasn't wearin them, and she had no idea where Jessica would have put them. Austin's mind ran a hundred miles an hour as he thought about where those two things could be since she wasn't wearin them, but Austin just assumed that the guy had taken them off of her and pawned them for money.

In the days after the funeral Austin's mother noticed how much Austin was strugglin so she wrote a letter to Rosanna Aydelotte hopin that she would write him back. In her letter his mother explained to Rosanna what had happened, and how Austin could use a friend. Austin's mother told her that he loved to watch her television show, and could she maybe get the cast to sign pictures and send them to him.

Two days before Christmas a big envelope arrived from New York. She ran up to Austin's room and gave it to him and said, "You have a letter from New York City."

"I don't know anyone from New York City." Austin said, as he took the big envelope from her. "What did you do?"

"Read the letter and then tell me if you're mad."

Austin ripped open the huge envelope and found pictures of all the cast from Americana. There were even a couple of things that only the cast got durin the holiday shows that were signed too. Then Austin found the letter inside, so he opened the letter and started to read it, it read;

Dear Austin,

I am sorry to hear about what happened to friend Jessica, and I wish there was more I could do to help you. I don't normally personally write back to fans, but there was somethin about your letter that touched me. I've had some of the cast sign photos for you, and sent a few things that only the cast gets when it comes to the holidays. I hope that you will keep writin me so that you can tell me all about your life, and keep me informed when it comes to findin out what really happened to Jessica.

Your friend,
Rosanna

"Austin, I saw how down you were, and I wrote a letter to her just hopin that she would send somethin back to you." Austin'smother explained, with a very big smile.

Austin didn't say anything just got off the bed and gave his mother a hug. He was so grateful that his mother cared about him that much to write a letter to his favorite actress wantin her to help him through such a rough time.

Nineteen ninety-three turned into nineteen ninety-four, and soon it was Valentine's Day. After school that day Austin's grandma took him to the flower shop in town, and he bought Jessica's favorite flowers calla lilies. Austin's grandma then took him and the rest of the grandkids out the cemetery where he could put them in the vase. That evenin Austin got out the scrapbook that he and Jessica had started and looked through it many times. He would always stop on the pages where they had written their weddin vows the year before. Austin would read them, and then start to cry because he knew he would never say those vows to her. He would laugh as he thought about how they had their lives all planned out. In that moment Austin decided that he wasn't goin to chase after his dreams anymore because it wouldn't be the same without Jessica there beside him.

On a chilly early March Sunday afternoon around one o' clock Austin and Jaelyn were sittin upstairs on the couch in the game room. Austin's mother had invited Jaelyn's family over for lunch because it had been a while since Jaelyn had been over to the house. As Jaedyn set two steps lower than the landin, she waited to hear a piece of information she could take back to the girls. Jaelyn had noticed the ring on Austin's right hand way back in December of ninety-two, and she didn't know why he was wearin it. After makin a little small talk Jaelyn asked, "Austin, why do you wear that ring on your right hand?"

"It's the promise ring that Jessica gave me the Christmas of nineteen ninety-two." Austin explained, as he lifted it up and looked at it.

"Did you give her one?"

"Yes, I did."

"So, you two promised that you would get married one day?"

"Yes, we did." Austin replied, holdin back his tears.

"How could the two of you know at such a young age?"

"I knew at age eight she and I were meant to be together, but I don't know when she realized it."

"Wow!" Jaelyn said, crackin a big smile as she looked at him. in the back of her mind Jaelyn hoped that one day Austin would be puttin a weddin ring on her finger.

On the stairs Jaedyn didn't realize that was the reason why Austin had been wearin that ring. All of his friends just thought that maybe it was his grandpa's, and that's why he was wearin it.

The spring came and went pretty quickly, and before we knew it school was almost ready to get out for summer. One mid-May afternoon after school, Lane was walkin to her grandma's house from the junior high while Austin had track practice. She cut through the neighbor's yard on Logan Street one street over from her grandma's house. As she stepped up on the brick walk at the edge of the property, she turned back and saw an odd yellow brown striped van go down Logan Street. She found it a little odd because she had never seen that kind of van in town before. Deep down in her spirit there was a sigh of relief that she was on the brick and not just then startin to walk across the neighbor's extra lot.

School got out and the summer had finally started. Austin spent most of the summer hangin out with his cousins, but he did spend time out at the Somerled Farm ridin horses with Jaelyn. Austin, Jaelyn, and Jaedyn all hung out together, and by the end of the summer Jaedyn understood Austin in a way that she never had before. She had made the decision not to tell Reese or Hope anything else about him because she didn't want them to take advantage of her friend.

By the time the Georgetown Fair came that year everyone in town thought that Austin and Jaelyn were datin because they were always together. Jaedyn didn't tell Reese or Hope whether it was the truth or not because she didn't think she had to tell them anything. Reese and Hope watched as Austin played the fair games, And he won Jaelyn all sorts of prizes. He even won her a goldfish to take home, and Jaelyn named it Roy. Reese, Hope, and the rest of the girls that liked Austin did notice that Austin hadn't taken the ring off of his right-hand ring finger. They just assumed that Jaelyn wasn't as special to him as she thought she was because of the ring on his right hand.

The nineteen ninety-four nineteen ninety-five school year started the followin Monday. It was Lane's freshman year in high school, and she was in the same mindset she had been in every year. And no surprise classmates were bullyin her not too many days after school started. Lane just tried to block it out by gettin lost in her stories that she was writin. Lane did find a bright spot in all the darkness as she quickly developed a crush on Mr. Somerled because to her he was so cute. He was tall, had dark brown hair, and his eyes seemed talk to you whenever he looked at you.. Austin was joined by Harley and Jaelyn that year in the junior high.

When September came many of Austin's friends wondered how he was goin to act because it had been a year since Jessica had been abducted and killed. On the twentieth Austin was very quiet, but Jaelyn tried her best just to be there for him. She really didn't know what else she could do, and it helped that they had the same lunch hour. Austin's mother had called the school, and asked them to keep an eye on him. She told them to call her if they thought that Austin needed to be sent home.

As October came the police still hadn't caught the person who had taken Jessica the year before. Hope and Eileen were out ridin their bikes on a warm October afternoon not far from Eileen's house when they noticed a yellow brown van followin them. Feelin very uncomfortable the two started to ride their bikes a little faster, and they made it back to Eileen's house. After calmin down the two called Hope's parents, and the four of them drove around town until they found the van. They took the license plate number down and reported to the police. In doin that the two girls help cracked Jessica's case wide open. A vermillion county detective went over to the state the van registered to talk to the men. After makin small talk the detective put Jessica's photo in front of the man. The man flinched very quickly when he saw the picture, and the detective knew he had the right person. That December Jessica's kidnapper was charged with kidnappin Jessica, and it went to a higher court to make sure there would be a conviction.

With Jessica's kidnapper in jail everyone one in the small communities started to sleep a little better, but still were aware that anything could happen in a small town. The thinkin they had for years that it could never happen in Georgetown had been shattered because it had happened and it rocked the town to the core. The innocencethe town had held for so many years was gone, and they would never get it back again.

On a cold snowy December afternoon Austin decided to write a letter to Rosanna Aydelotte to let her know what was happenin with Jessica's case. He wrote the letter about five times before he was finally happy with what he had written. The letter read;

Dear Rosanna,

I wanted to let you know that they have found Jessica's killer and have charged him. They haven't set a trial date, but I'm goin every day to be there as a representative of her. I'm so glad that that man is behind bars and cannot hurt anyone else. I hope things are goin good on the set of Americana, and that you're enjoy filmin each new show. I don't want to take too much of your time, so I will write you another letter when I have some news.

Your fan,

Austin Reid

As nineteen ninety-four ended and nineteen ninety-five started, Austin was strummin his guitar, but really didn't have the heart to play it because it felt hollow without Jessica there to play to. As he played the last chord, and started to put the guitar up in its stand, the tall silhouette leanin up against the door and said, "Don't put it up. I love to hear you play your guitar and sing."

"I really don't feel like it, sweetness." Austin replied, as he looked over at her.

"Are you ever goin to play your guitar for me?" Jaelyn asked, as she walked from the doorway over to the bed and sat down.

"Maybe one of these days."

"Someday soon I hope."

"Maybe?" Austin replied, as he cracked his boyish grin.

As Jaelyn looked around the room she had noticed that he had put pictures of the two of them up around his side of the room next to pictures of him and Jessica. With a big smile she said, "I must be very special to you because you have my pictures up in your room."

"You are."

"I am.." Jaelyn said, with a big smile excited to hear that she Austin thought she was special.

"You are.." Austin replied, seein that spark in her eyes he saw years ago.

Jaelyn just looked at him with the biggest smile, and a few seconds later she startin runnin out of the room. Austin soon got up and was runnin right behind her. The two made their way downstairs in the livin room through the kitchen and out the back door. Austin's mother watched and was reminded of when he and Jessica used to do that all the time. She started to wonder if maybe Jaelyn would be more than a friend to him at some point in his life.

As nineteen ninety-five started the world was full of great expectations and excitement as people around the world wondered what the new year would bring. The year started off with a scientist in Hawaii discoverin the farthest galaxy away from earth. Russia set the space endurance record. Marines deploy into Somalia. Bill Clinton delivers his state of the union address, and the San Frisco 49ers win their fifth super bowl.

In my own life I couldn't wait for the last half of the school year to get over, and for summer to be here where I could be free from homework. Eloise and I had broke up because she wanted to focus on her dancin because she told me it would be her future. Beverly and Christine were still askin everyone in town, and on the farm about Benjamin and his story. A few people told them of Benjamin's younger days, but wouldn't talk about any other period in his life. Lee Ann started talkin to me, and we seemed to have a lot in common. We seemed to like a lot of the same things which surprised me a little.

That February Lee Ann and I went to the Valentine's Day dance together at school. Eloise pretended that she wasn't upset, but I could tell that she didn't like me hangin out with one of her best friends. Up in Illinois Austin and Jaelyn went to the Valentine's Day dance together at their junior high school. Many of their classmates were surprised that Austin would actually go to the dance at all.

As the song "Someone Else's Star" by Bryan White played, Austin and Jaelyn were on the gym floor slowin dancin together. As the two looked into each other's eyes Jaelyn asked, "Cupcake, will you ever date again?"

"I don't know." Austin replied, crackin his boyish grin.

"So you are goin to be alone for the rest of your life?"

"I don't want to be alone, but I need some time to process that my future doesn't include Jessica anymore. Why?"

"I was just wonderin is all." Jaelyn said, crackin her smile as she put her arms around his neck.

"When I do decide to date anyone you will be the first to know." Austin explained, as he pulled her closer to him.

Everyone at the dance saw them dancin and wondered how Jaelyn got Austin to move forward from Jessica so quickly. They all knew that Jaelyn would probably be the girl he would be with for the rest of his life now. They couldn't believe that how quickly Austin had let someone back into his heart after losin Jessica just a year ago. It didn't take long for it to be in the gossip mill around the small town.

Five weeks later spring finally arrived, and the last nine weeks of school went by so quickly. We were out for summer break, and just bein kids again not havin to worry about homework. Austin spent most of his summer out on his grandparent's farm because his grandpa wanted to teach him about the Farm equipment because he would be workin on the farm soon enough. I spent most of my days with my grandparents takin little adventures all around Mississippi and Alabama.

That June the trial of Jessica's kidnapper started, and Austin and his parents were there every day. Jessica's family and many of her friends were there too, and let the man who took her know that she was important. The trial only took eight days before it went to the jury. When the jury came back to give the verdict they had come to everyone in the courtroom was on the edge of their seat. When the jury foreman read the verdict the court irrupted in joy because the man was convicted of kidnappin for purposes of sexual gratification. Austin smiled from ear to ear for days because that guy got what he deserved.

That August Austin was with the Roth family when the man was sentenced to life in prison without the possibility of parole. Austin felt a weight lift off of his shoulders because the man had been caught and was payin for his did to his childhood sweetheart. Austin still felt the weight that he had put on himself for not bein there to protect her from that evil man.

Before we knew all of us were sittin back in a classroom. We were lookin out the window wantin so much to be outside enjoyin the summer weather. Austin joined Lane at the high school that school year. Eloise, Lee Ann Beverly, me, and the rest of our group also started high school that year. We were freshmen and wondered if we could make it the next four years. I joined the football team and was good enough to play on the varsity team, and up in Illinois Austin had joined the football team. He was also good enough to play on the varsity team. The GRHS football team hoped that they would have another dream season like they had the year before goin all the way to Bloomington to play at state.

When Austin found a little time to just sit down, he wrote a letter

to Rosanna to let her know what was goin on with Jessica's case.

He wanted to her to know that the kidnapper had been found guilty,

and was goin to spend his life in prison where he couldn't hurt anybody

else. At the same time Austin was writin his letter across the street

Jessica's father was gettin into her mustang to get the title out of it

because the family had decided to sell it rather than keep it. As he looked

through the glovebox he found a folded piece of paper that he hadn't seen

in there before, and wantin to know what it was he opened it and read it. It

read;

Dear Austin,

If you are readin this it means that I am on an air force base

somewhere in this country or abroad.. I know that you will soon be gettin

your license and will be able to drive where you want to go. I also know that

your father isn't goin to give you a car to drive right after gettin them. I know

my dad would rather have my car stay in the garage where he can drive it

every now and then, but I've told him to give it to you so you'll have a piece

of me while I'm away. Then when I come home we can make more

memories in it. Please take good care of my car, and please don't wreck it

or I will have to hurt you.

Love Always

Jessica

As he read the letter tears came for his eyes, and he knew that he would have to give the car to Austin because Jessica wanted him to have it. The car wasn't ready to be driven because it still needed some work done to it. Jessica's father took the letter in to show his wife, and after she read it the two talked about it. After much discussion Jessica's parents decided to give the car to Austin but not tell him about the letter. A few days later Jessica's parents walked over to Austin's house and had a discussion with Austin's parents, and the four came to an agreement for Austin to have the car. He would have to help fix it up with Jessica's father before he could have it.

As the hot days of summer turned into chilly nights, Austin would go to Jessica's house every day after football practice. Since the last time he had seen the car Austin noticed that all the seats had green seat covers. He smiled as he thought about how Jessica was determined to make the car her own with little touches of her favorite color. Austin would sit in the driver's seat just like Jessica used to do, and he would close his eyes and try to picture her sittin in the seat next to him with the biggest smile on her face.

That September twentieth Austin had his grandma take him to
the flower shop to get cala lilies to put in the vase of her headstone.
His grandma then drove him out to the cemetery, and she watched
as Austin put the flowers in the vase. Then he played his guitar and
sang the song "Always Have, Always Will" to her because even
though she was no longer with him his heart would always be hers.

A few weeks later it was time for the Sadie Hawkins dance
at the high school, and many of the girls had already asked Austin
to go to the dance with them but he had said no. Then on a very
chilly Wednesday mornin Austin was settin at a cafeteria table
when a tall average blonde curly headed teenage girl walked up
and set down beside him. As she cracked a big smile she asked,
"Austin Reid, will you go to the dance with me?"

"I don't think so, Reese." Austin replied, as he looked over at her
with a grin.

"Why not?"

"Because I just don't feel like I should."

"Why?"

"I'm still not over Jessica yet, and it wouldn't be fair to you."

"Austin, it's just dancin." Reese said, with a giggle and a smile.

"I'm not askin you to go out with me. I just want to dance with you and have a little fun."

"Let me think about it." Austin said, as he cracked his boyish grin. "And I will let you know."

As the bell rang for school to start that mornin, Reese got up from the table and with a big grin said, "Ok, let me know your answer."

Austin went to the dance with Reese that Friday night and he did have fun just dancin. He danced with Hope and a few other girls which made Reese a little jealous. Austin wasn't on a date with him so he really didn't care. Peyton, Maddy, Hope, Eileen and a few other girls couldn't believe that Reese got Austin to go out with her to the dance. The girls thought that maybe Austin had decided to finally move forward with his life, and move forward with Reese and not Jaelyn.

Austin went to every volleyball game at the junior high from August to October to support Jaelyn. Jaelyn would go to every football game home or away to support Austin just as he did her.

Reese along with the other girls in town were jealous that Jaelyn had Austin's full attention and she got to wear his opposite jersey to all of his football games. The girls thought it wasn't fair because Jaelyn wasn't even in high school she was just an seventh grader.

The holiday season seemed to come quick that year and we were soon on Christmas vacation. As the new year started everyone was filled with excitement for what ninety-six would bring. That February Jessica's kidnapper's attorney argued that he deserved a new trial because he didn't get a fair durin the first trial. Jessica's family, Austin, and friends waited to hear the judges rulin on the appeal which made their year start off a little shaky. Austin found the key to his parent's liquor cabinet in the dinin room, and he started to steal a bottle every now and then. His parents would wonder where the bottle went because the key was always in its place, and they hadn't caught any of their children with the bottle.

On Valentine's Day that year Austin went out to eat and to the mall with Jaelyn. They went to the local pizza joint Jocko's, and then went out to the village mall to look around and shop. The two spent a lot of the time in the toy store just lookin at all the different toys along with playin with some of them that were out of the boxes. The two were actin silly and many people in the toy store saw the two of them playin around like little kids. One shopper in the store even said to his wife. How fun it would be to go back to that age and be so much in love again, Austin heard the remark but didn't really think about it. Jaelyn, on the other hand, took the comment to heart because she had fallen in love with Austin but was too shy to tell him.

Spring came slowly as the end of the school year came into view. Austin and Jessica's family's life were still up in the air as they still waited for the rulin the judge had made on her kidnapper's appeal. Austin decided to run track that spring to keep his mind busy since he and Jessica's dad had finally gotten the car runnin. While runnin around town for track practice, Austin seemed to let his guard down and actually talked to Reese.

That summer flew by too quickly, and before the kids in Illinois could blink that Georgetown Fair was in town. Reese was expectin Austin to spend some time at the fair with her, but she was disappointed because he went to the fair every night with Jaelyn. To the people in town Austin had moved on from Jessica with Jaelyn, and the towns' people were happy to see him happy again. The fair week went way fast, and the nineteen ninety-six – ninety-seven school year started.

A few weeks after that a judge vacated Jessica's kidnapper's conviction and ordered a new trial which turned Austin and Jessica's family worlds upside down. A few days after that Austin started gettin into his parent's liquor cabinet and drinkin very heavily. Even though he knew that he could talked to Jaelyn about what was goin on he decided to write a letter to Rosanna to tell her what had happened in Jessica's case.

On hot August Wednesday New York mornin Rosanna got home from her daily run, and she sat down on the couch ran her fingers through her shoulder length blonde corkscrew curly hair her mother walked into the livin room and said, "I forgot to give you this letter from Austin yesterday after you came home from work."

"I haven't heard from Austin in a long time, so somethin must have happened." Rosanna replied, as she ripped open the envelope.

"When was the last time you heard from him?" Rosanna's mother replied, as she sat down in the chair across from her daughter.

"After the man was convicted of kidnappin Jessica and he was sentenced to life in prison."

"So just over a year since you've heard from him."

"Yes, I think so." Rosanna said, as she unfolded the piece of paper and started to read it out loud. The letter read;

Dear Rosanna,

I hope that this letter does fine you well. I know it's been such a long time since I've written to you, but my life has been busy with school and all. I'm enjoyin the new season of Americana, and can't wait to see how the season ends. I writin you today because a judge has just vacated the verdict of Jessica's kidnapper, and he will get another trial. So I, her family, and friends will all have to set through another trial, and hope that the next jury that hears the evidence will always come back with the same verdict as the first one. I don't know when the trial will be, but I know that I will be there every day representin Jessica and the life that she didn't get to finish livin. I hope I didn't bring you down, and I hope the rest of this year is good for you. Just wanted to let you know what was goin on in my life right now.

Your friend,

Austin.

By the look on her daughter's face she could tell somethin was wrong, so before Rosanna could say anything her mother asked, "Ro, what's wrong?"

"A judge vacated Jessica's kidnapper's verdict and he's gettin another trial." Rosanna replied, as she looked up at her mother.

"I bet that boy is all tied up in knots and angry."

"I wish I could do somethin for him then just send another letter to him."

"Maybe we can." Rosanna's mother replied, with a grin as she got up to walk out of the room.

"What are you thinkin? Mother, what are you up to?" Rosanna asked, as she jumped off the couch and followed her mother into the kitchen.

The hot summer days slowly turned into chilly September nights. Austin went to Jaelyn's volleyball games, but she could tell that his mind was somewhere else. She was just happy that he was there to support her through the rough time he was goin through. Jaelyn did notice at the football games Austin seemed to be puttin all of his anger in hittin someone from the other team when the football would be snapped.

Before the high school kids knew in Illinois was homecomin week again, and it was the week of the third anniversary of Jessica's abduction. Everyone could tell that with what the judge had done, and the anniversary Austin was havin a rough week. Hope and a few others tried to help him throughout the week, but he wouldn't talk or listen to any of them. Austin stayed home on Saturday night, and didn't even go to the homecomin dance. Instead, he got into his parent's liquor cabinet, got a bottle of vodka, and walked over to Jessica's house. He got the key to the garage from its hidin spot and made his way into the garage walkin over to the car. He spent the next few hours drinkin the vodka until it hit him so hard he fell asleep in the backseat. After he was sleepin very sound when he felt someone pushin on his nose, in his dream Austin opened up his eyes and he saw Jessica leanin over the driver's seat smilin and laughin as she pushed his nose down. Austin just stared at her for a few minutes and then asked, "What do you think you're doin?"

"Wakin you up." Jessica replied, with a big smile. "We need to have a talk."

"Really?" Austin said, as he set up in the backseat lookin into her lovin blue eyes.

"You can't quit singin and playin your guitar, Austin. It's your future."

"But with you not here, I really don't want to chase after my dreams. I haven't played in the talent show since you've been gone."

"You have real talent, Austin Reid, and the world needs to see it."

"Jessi, please.. I don't think I can do it without you here by my side."

"I will be by your side." Jessica said, as he started to run her fingers through his hair. "I've never left you, but you have to be patient and watch the miracle unfold in front of you."

"What miracle?" Austin asked, a little confused by her statement.

"I can't go into detail but just believe that a miracle can happen."

"Ok, satnin.. I will believe that a miracle can happen."

"Are you fallin for Jaelyn, Austin?"

"I'm not fallin for Jaelyn." Austin replied, very quickly.

"Sunshine, it's alright." Jessica said, as she crossed her arms and put her head on them as she looked into Austin's ice blue eyes.

Austin cracked his boyish grin and said, "She and I are just friends. I can talk to her about anything just like we used to talk."

"I'm glad you can talk to her, but I know that you're fallin in love with her."

"You know I will never stop lovin you, Jessica." Austin said, as he kissed her on the nose. "I'm startin to move forward with my life."

"I know." Jessica said, with a big smile. "And soon will come the day when you will have to decide whether you want to be with her or me."

Austin couldn't say anything because he was so dumbfounded by what Jessica had said to him. He took the last drink of vodka out of the bottle and fell back asleep in the back seat of the car.

On Sunday mornin when Jessica's father went out to get the family car for church he walked past the mustang and saw Austin lyin in the back seat with an empty bottle of vodka in the floorboard. Jessica's father called Austin's parents and told them about findin Austin in the garage. Austin's father grounded him for two months, and he hoped that Austin wouldn't be that stupid again.

The holiday season came quickly that year, and it was almost Thanks-givin before we knew it. Everyone around the world was gettin ready for it by doin the meal prep a few days ahead of time. At Austin's house his mother had pulled the entire family in to help prep the vegetables and other things because it was their turn to host the celebration. Everyone knew that their great uncle from Brocton would bring a few exchange students that were goin to the college in Charleston.

On Tuesday evenin, Austin was peelin and cuttin apples for his mother's famous apple pie, and his brother and sister were snappin fresh green beans. His father was at the stove stirrin a pot when there was a knock at the door. With a big smile Austin's mother said, "Austin, can you get the door."

"Sure.." Austin said, jumpin up from the dinin room table. He made his way to the front door, and as he opened the door he was shocked to see who was standin at his front door. "Rosanna Aydelotte, what are you doin here?"

"Surprise!" Rosanna replied, with a big smile on her face. "My family and I decided to spend the holiday with your family."

"Really?"

"Your mother didn't tell you?"

"No, she didn't tell me." Austin said, crackin his boyish grin. "I guess she wanted it to be a surprise. What made you decide to spend the holiday with me and my family?"

"Can we come in? It's a little chilly out here."

"Of course."

"I got your letter tellin me that Jessica's kidnapper got a new trial and I wanted to do more than just write you a letter back."

"So that's why I never got a letter back."

"Yes." Rosanna replied, with a big smile gigglin. "My mother and I had our agent track where you lived and your phone number. I called and talked to your mother and we come up with us spendin the holiday with you. Give you somethin to smile about instead of bein sad."

"Thank you, it was just the surprise I needed." Austin replied, crackin his boyish grin.

Over the next few hours both families visited and got to know each other, but Brandon and Rosanna's brother Wyatt soon went upstairs to play video games. Just before sunset Austin and Rosanna went out on the back porch because she needed a cigarette, and couldn't smoke in the house. Austin turned on the radio that was sittin on the table. It wasn't long before the two were dancin to music without a care in the world. Rosanna looked up at Austin, put her arms around his neck and passionately kissed him. Austin ran his hand down her back to her waist

On the deck next door Hope, Reese, Eileen, Peyton, Maddy, Jaedyn, Jaelyn, and a few other friends of theirs were talkin when they noticed what was happenin on Austin's porch. Breakin the silence Peyton looked over at Reese and asked, "Who is that woman Austin is kissin?"

"I have no idea who that woman is." Reese replied, as she watched Austin kiss the mystery woman.

"How could he do that?" Jaelyn said, gettin very upset with what she saw.

"Did you know that he was talkin to someone else, Jaelyn?" Hope asked, knowin that Jaelyn was upset.

"No, I didn't know he was talkin to anyone else."

"Maybe she's a long distant friend who is only visitin for the holiday." Jaedyn said, as she looked at her sister.

"I can't believe he would do that." Jaelyn said, a little heartbroken that Austin would be kissin someone else.

"Well, better to learn now than be surprised later when he tells everyone he is datin someone." Eileen said, with a laugh knowin it was stingin a little hard for a few people.

"Jaelyn, are you all right?"

"I'll be all right." Jaelyn said, as she wiped tears from both of her eyes.

The girls just watched as Austin and Rosanna made out with each other a little more. Jaelyn was still wipin tears from her eyes because she couldn't believe that Austin would treat her so coldly. She remembered him sayin that if he was goin to start datin she would be the first know. It was at that point Hope gave up ever tryin to win Austin's attention, and she was goin to give the other boys in town a chance.

The next day around two o'clock Rosanna was on her third cup of coffee and Austin was still in bed sleepin. She really didn't understand why he wanted to sleep so much of the day away. As the kids ran through the livin room Rosanna said, "I can't wait any longer I'm goin to go upstairs and wake Austin up."

"Ok, Ro." Her mother said, as she looked over at her.

"He won't wake up easy you'll have to shake him." Austin's mother said, knowin full well that he doesn't wake up easily.

Rosanna made her way up the stairs to the room Austin shared with his younger brother. As she opened the door Rosanna she found Austin sittin on his bed strummin his guitar. As she made her way inside the room she looked around at all the pictures on Austin's side. She saw pictures of him with Jessica all over his dressers and the nightstand beside his bed. Rosanna also saw picture of Austin with another young girl that by her smile reminded you of Jessica because the smile was so bright. Rosanna also saw just how much of an Elvis Presley fan Austin was with his movie posters and other Elvis related things around his room. As she leaned up against the dresser she said, "So who is this girl in the pictures with you?"

"Just a friend." Austin said, as he looked up from his guitar.

"So are you finally movin forward with your life from Jessica?"

"I think I'm beginnin to.."

"So the two of you are just friends?." Rosanna said, as she walked over and set down on the bed beside him.

"Yes, we are just friends."

"Are you goin to ask this young girl out anytime soon?"

"I thought about maybe at Christmas or New Year's."

"That would be the perfect gift to give her."

"Yes, I think so." Austin replied, crackin his boyish grin.

"Why don't you play me somethin on that guitar of yours." Rosanna said, with a big smile. "Your mother was tellin us what a good guitar player you are and that you sing too."

"I do, but I haven't really played since Jessica was killed."

"It's all right just take your time. Remember I have the next three days."

After about twenty minutes Austin finally got the courage to strum the first chord and sing his first note in front of a person that wasn't Jessica. After the song was over Rosanna smiled from ear to ear and said, "Austin Reid, I do believe that you can be a star in the future."

"You think so?" Austin asked, as he cracked his boyish grin.

"Yes, I do. And I'll have my parents talk to our family's agent Isabella Zimbalist so she can represent when you're ready."

"Really?" Austin asked, crackin his boyish grin.

"Yes."

"I thought about not chasin after my dreams because without Jessica it just seems empty."

"She would proud of you if you did." Rosanna said, tryin to help him see how good he is.

A few hours later Rosanna was tellin Austin all about her journey to becomin a star in the eyes of everyone in the world. She told him that it wasn't an easy trip to go on, and it would take a lot of work. Rosanna also told him it would take a lot of determination on his part to.

On Thanksgivin mornin Rosanna helped the ladies in the kitchen, as they started cookin the meal for that afternoon. Lane and Harley couldn't believe that she was gettin to meet Rosanna Aydelotte and her family. She was an actress that Lane had looked up to for many years. Austin's grandmothers were very impressed that not only was Rosanna, her mother, and grandmother were all learnin from them, but the three of them were also teachin Austin's grandmothers and aunts too.

When both families set down to eat Thanksgivin dinner Austin's grand-father said grace before the meal was passed around. It wasn't long before the stories of yesterday were bein told on Grandpa Reid and other family members. Soon Rosanna's family were sharin stories of their own about some funny moments that had happened in their family over the years. There were a few stories that Rosanna had never heard before which she found very interestin.

After eatin Thanksgivin dinner Austin decided to call Jaelyn, and wish her a happy Thanksgivin. Deep down he was hopin that she would be happy to hear from him since it had been almost a four days since they had last talked to each other. After talkin to her grandmother for a few minutes she finally handed the phone over to Jaelyn and Austin said, "Happy Thanksgivin, Sweetness."

"Happy Thanksgivin, Austin." Jaelyn said, in a very upset tone as she looked over at her sister.

"Is everything all right?"

"Everything is fine, I guess. You forgot to tell me that you finally decided to move forward from Jessica and start datin."

"Oh no, that hasn't happened." Austin said, a little confused as he looked at Rosanna who was leanin up against the kitchen island. "What gave you that idea?"

"I saw you."

"You saw me what?"

"I saw you kiss that girl that's at your house for the holiday." Jaelyn said, upset as tears fell from her eyes.

"I'm not datin her..." Austin said, with a laugh. "You've got the wrong idea."

"You think it's funny?"

"It was just a little dare I didn't think that she would do it."

"A dare? You expect me to believe that?"

"Yes, Sweetness, I do." Austin replied, knowin that he was lyin through his teeth.

"I don't believe you." Jaelyn said, before she slammed the phone down in his ear. She wiped tears from her eyes as she walked back into the livin room with her family upset that Austin had the nerve to talk to her after what he had done.

Austin spent the last three days Rosanna was in town tellin her all about Jessica, and the life they had dreamed about livin when they got older. He told her about the silliest and the saddest times they had together. He showed her pictures of the two of them when they were very young to the last pictures of them together before the tragedy happened. Rosanna told Austin about some of her funniest moments on the different sets she had worked on. She also told him stories from the set of Americana, and Austin felt so special to have Rosanna's friendship.

The last night that Rosanna and her family were in town Austin and Rosanna were in her room talkin about Americana and what she wanted to do in the future. Then out of the blue Rosanna leaned over and gave Austin a passionate kiss on the lips. It wasn't long before Austin and Rosanna were lyin on the bed makin out. As she looked down into his ice blue eyes and ran her fingers through his hair she said, "Do you what to...?"

"I've never had.." Austin explained, as he looked up into her enchantin blue green eyes.

"It's ok. We'll take it slow."

"Are you sure?"

Rosanna just cracked a big as she put her arm around his neck and passionately kissed him. It wasn't long before the two forgot about what was happenin outside of Rosanna's bedroom because they were so focused on each other.

Two hours later as the sun started to set outside Austin and Rosanna were lyin in her bed just starin into each other's eyes when Austin said, "I didn't realize that sex was that fun."

"Oh, yes." Rosanna replied, with a big smile and laugh. "It's a lot of fun."

"You bein here as really helped me a lot because I found out you're just a normal person just like me."

"It's too bad that you already have a girlfriend otherwise I would love to be." Rosanna said, as she ran her fingers through his hair.

"Maybe, sometime in the future there will be a you and I."

"Until then." Rosanna said, as she gave him a kiss. "I'm goin to take advantage of the time I have with you."

"You better.."

"What about Jaelyn?"

"This may only happen once in my life, so I'm goin to take advantage of it too." Austin said, crackin his boyish grin as he gave her a kiss.

Early Sunday mornin Rosanna and her family made their way back to the airport in Indianapolis to catch a plane home to New York City. After gettin back to the city Rosanna called Austin to let his family know that They had made it safely back home. Rosanna told Austin that she was to few scripts from Americana so that he could look at them and see if he remembered the episode.

Before we could blink it was Christmas time all over the world. Austin had been tryin to talk to Jaelyn for the last three weeks, but she ' wouldn't talk to him at all. He even sent her a letter but it was sent back return to sender unopened. Austin wasn't goin to give up because he really wanted to talk to her because he knew that if she listened to ' Jaedyn, Reese or Hope their relationship would be over before it started.

On Sunday December twenty second the church had a Christmas party after church that mornin. Everyone was eatin what people had brought in for the potluck dinner, and visitin with each other. Austin did everything he could to get close to Jaelyn, but she would move away from him. Even after Jaedyn told him to leave her sister alone he still tried to talk to her. When Austin saw Jaelyn headin toward the door to walk out of the fellowship hall. Austin ran over to the door and followed her down the stairs. As he tried to catch up with her Austin said, "Sweetness, stop we need to talk."

"I don't want to talk to you." Jaelyn replied, as she looked back at him as she made her way into the sanctuary.

"Please, we need to talk."

"Won't your girlfriend be mad at you for talkin to me?"

"I don't know." Austin said, crackin his boyish grin. "My girlfriend is standin right in front of me."

"What?" Jaelyn asked, with a little smile and blushin. "I'm your girl-friend?"

"Yes, if you want to be. That's what I wanted to talk to you about."

"You want me to be your girlfriend?"

"Sweetness, you know I do."

"What about that woman who was at your house over Thanksgivin?"

"I've explained that you all ready. It was just a dare, and I didn't think she would actually do it. "

After walkin over to where Austin was standin Jaelyn asked, "So I am the first one to know that you are ready to date again?"

"Yes, Sweetness, you are."

"And you really want to go out with me?"

As he took her hand and the two set down in a pew, Austin looked into her green eyes and said, "Yes, I really want to go out with you."

"I really thought that you had moved on with that woman who was at your house on Thanksgivin." Jaelyn said, with a serious look in her bright green eyes.

"No, you assumed wrong, Sweetness."

"So you really want me to be your girlfriend?"

"Yes, I do." Austin said, as he cracked his boyish grin.

Jaelyn smiled from ear to ear as she leaned over, and gave Austin a kiss on the cheek. The two then made their way back upstairs walkin hand in hand surprisin many people up in the fellowship hall.

The new year came Austin was so happy because he got to be in driver's ed class that semester. He could finally learn how to drive and finally have the freedom he's always wanted to have. that way his father wouldn't have to know everything he was doin. The snow in January let the kids in the Georgetown school district had many snow days that month. February came and so did the Valentine's Day dance at the high school, and Austin wasn't surprised when a lot of the girls asked him to go to the dance with them and he said no.

With snow fallin down outside on a cold February mornin Austin was standin at his locker when Reese walked up to the locker andsaid, "Austin, go to the Valentine's dance with me?"

"Reese," Austin said, as he put his books in his locker. "I'm not goin to go with you to the dance."

"Who are you goin with?"

"I'm not goin with anyone."

"Austin, you have to go to the dance it will be fun."

"Reese, I'm goin to the Valentine's dance with Jaelyn at the junior high that night.."

"Why?" Reese asked, as she leaned up against the lockers.

"Because she asked me to go" Austin explained, as he shut his locker.

"You're goin to a junior high dance when you're in high school? Why?"

"Because I want to, and I can do whatever I want to."

"Oh well." Reese said, with a big grin as she walked away from him. "You'll regret not goin with me.."

Austin just watched her walk down the hall as he shook his head. He realized that when Reese found out he was datin Jaelyn she would probably be upset because she wanted to date him so badly. Austin knew that she knew he and Jaelyn were close after seein him Holdin hands with Jaelyn at the Christmas party.

On Valentine's Day afternoon Austin's grandma Reid took Austin out to the cemetery after school, so he could put calla lilies in the vase of Jessica's headstone. Austin's grandma watched Austin talk to Jessica as he wiped his the tears from his eyes. She felt so sad for him because she knew deep down that he would never get over losin that young girl for the rest of his life.

On Friday night Jaelyn's parents picked up Austin around five o'clock that evenin. Austin gave Jaelyn a dozen red roses when he got into the car which impressed her parents. Jaelyn's father drove them to the junior high, and all four of them got out of the car because her parents were there to watch the teenagers at the dance along with a few other parents.

Austin and Jaelyn were dancin to a slow song, and as Austin looked deep into her eyes and saw the future he said, "Sweetness, I'm so glad that god brought you into my life."

"You know that there are goin to be a lot of mad people when they find out that we're datin." Jaelyn said, with a big smile and her green eyes shinin so bright.

Austin laughed as he looked into her bright green eyes, and enjoyin the mischievous smile on her face. He knew that the two were goin to have a lot of fun keepin their secret.

A few feet away Jaelyn's mother was watchin them because she wasn't too happy that Austin had an interest in her daughter. Mrs. Somerled thought he would only break her little girl's heart.

On a chilly March afternoon Austin had gotten on the bus to go to the track meet at another school. He was sittin by himself when a tall skinny curly blonde-haired girl set down beside him and said, "What are you doin?"

"I'm just sittin here, Reese." Austin replied, as he cracked his boyish smile.

As she set down beside him in the seat Reese asked, "Reidsy, are you ever goin to date anyone new, or are you goin to be single forever?"

"I don't know, I haven't decided yet."

"Really? Then why do you spend a lot of time at Jaedyn's house with her little sister?"

"Jaelyn and I are friends." Austin replied, crackin his boyish grin.

"Why are you so interested in when I'm goin to date again?"

"Reidsy, I really like you and I was hopin that you liked me. I know that if you just gave us a chance we would be so good together." Reese explained, with a big smile.

"You really think so?"

Reese's smile got bigger as she leaned over and gave him a some-what of a passionate kiss. Right in the middle of that kiss Peyton, Maddy, and Dawn walked onto the bus findin them in that intimate moment. With a huge smile and laugh Peyton asked, "Well, look what we have here."

"I think Reese finally got her boy. "Maddy said, as she set down in a seat.

"That's enough," Austin said, as he stopped kissin Reese. "What do you mean?"

"The two of you are datin now right?" Dawn asked, with a big grin joinin in the conversation.

"We are not datin. Reese just kissed me for no reason at all."

"But you kissed her back, so you must like her." Maddy said, with a point.

"I do.."

"Then, just go out with her already." Peyton said, with a big laugh and smile. "I get tired of hearin how much she wants you to be her boyfriend."

"That's not goin to happen because I'm still not ready to date yet." Austin replied, with a very serious look on his face.

"Well, I guess the two of you will just have fun until you decide to." Maddy said, with a big smile and laugh.

"We could?" Reese said, crackin a big smile as she looked over at him.

Austin just looked at all of them, and shook his head with a smile. Austin then sat back in his seat as the other members of the track team got on the bus. He cracked his boyish grin as he thought about how all the girls would react when they learned hewas datin Jaelyn. Austin knew that he shouldn't mess around with Reese because he was datin Jaelyn. Part of him thought it would be all right because no one knew the two of them were datin.

At the end of April Lane's doctor scheduled her surgery to break her jaw and move it up for the second week of July. Austin and Lane got to talkin and they decided to go on a summer adventure before she had her surgery. They decided to go to Saltillo, Mississippi for a few weeks, so that Austin could see Elvis Presley's childhood home in Tupelo. The cousin's parents were a bit reluctant because Lane was only seventeen and Austin would be sixteen. Plus, it was a nine-and-a-half-hour drive to Saltillo, and they didn't think the two should be doin it by themselves.

After a lot of discussion between all four parents decided to let them go, so the cousins could experience some life on their own. April finally turned into May, and the end of the school year couldn't come fast enough. When we finally got to have our summer break my mother told me that I had to get a job at the diner so I went and applied, and no surprise Mrs. Schlatter hired me. Lee Ann, Beverly, Christine, and Eloise were spendin the summer spendin money on things that they didn't need but wanted.

Up in Illinois on June sixth Austin finally turned sixteen, and his parents had a pool party for him with family and friends. Austin's last present was from Jessica's parents, and everyone was shocked when they gave him a nineteen sixty-five mustang with green seats and black interior. It had a personalized license plate with the words Satnin. Everyone soon found out that it was Jessica's car, and they wanted him to have it because that's what she would have wanted. Jaelyn was a little upset because there was somethin else that would remind Austin of Jessica. Just when Jaelyn thought that she had him all to herself Jessica came back into the picture once again, and Jaelyn wasn't sure that she could live with Jessica's ghost in their relationship all the time.

That evenin when there were just a handful of friends left at Austin's party. The group of friends were sittin around the table talkin about what they were goin to do that summer. They hadn't noticed that Austin and

Jaelyn were sittin on the edge of steps in the pool talkin to each other. As she sat next to him Jaelyn asked, "Cupcake, do you have to go to Mississippi with Lane?"

"I do, Sweetness." Austin said, as he looked over at her crackin his boyish grin.

"But I thought that we'd spend the summer together."

"I'll be gone for two weeks, and then I'll be back to spend the rest of the summer with you."

"Really?"

"Yes, really."

As she moved closer to him to where their lips were inches apart Jaelyn said, "Happy birthday.."

"Thank you." Austin said, crackin his boyish grin as he looked into her green eyes.

Jaelyn cracked a big smile as she leaned in and gave him a passionate kiss on the lips. The two kissed each other so long that it got the attention of his friends settin around the table. Reese and a few other girls at the party got jealous and upset. Austin's guy friends that were there just laughed as they watched the girls leave because they were upset that Austin was kissin another girl in front of them.

Chapter Three

The Summer

In Saltillo, Mississippi, I started my first job at Schlatter's Diner. I was a bus boy, dishwasher, and worked from the time I got there until the time I left. I did like that many of the regular customers would give me tips like five or ten dollars as they were leavin the table even though I hadn't waited on them. Everyone in this small town helped each other, and wanted to see the best happen. Schlatter's Diner was closed on Sunday, so everyone could go to church that mornin.

Sunday, June 22, was a day I'll never forget. We were runnin late for church so dad turned mom's red monte carlo into a race car tryin to get there on time. Just as Rev. Schlatter started his sermon we walked in and found our seats. It was nice that one of mom's co-workers would save some space in the pew. Rev. Schlatter got right down to the teachin of a particular scripture the lord had given him. This Sunday it was 1 Timothy 6: 6-8, "But godliness with contentment is great grain. For we brought nothin in this world, and we cannot take nothin out of it. But we have food and clothin we will be content with that."

After almost two hours, he finally ended his long sermon and we bowed our heads as he prayed, "Lord, please touch all the people who came this mornin, so they spread your love to strangers they meet. Bringin new souls into your kingdom. I ask this in Jesus name, amen."

As the quietness turned into chatter, I scanned the church for my friends. I wasn't surprised to see Eloise there with her parents. She was a tall skinny teenage girl with long blonde hair and intense dark brown eyes. I noticed that Eloise was talkin to Larlee Panko, a short thin elderly woman with a gracious spirit, and her daughter Jean Dunn. She was a tall average woman with short brunette hair and very sad brown eyes.

Walkin over there I saw her shake hands with two young strangers I'd never seen before. With curiosity and a smile, I walked up and said, "Good mornin ladies, how are you today?"

"We're fine, David," Larlee replied, given me a hug.

"Good to see you," Jean said, barin a little smile.

Just hearin my name was hard for her because she had lost her son David years ago. To this day everyone debates whether it was suicide or murder. She had never recovered from the tragic event, and she had spent years leanin on her mama until Mrs. Panko had to be strong for the two of them.

"David, I would like you to meet my great niece Lane Reid and her cousin Austin."

As we shook hands and said hello, I quickly figured out that they weren't from the south. Mrs. Panko told me that they were from the northern state of Illinois. There was a little small talk before I had to leave to go eat lunch at my grandparents' house.

Over the next few days, Austin and Lane settled into Larlee's house and she fed them well at each meal. From biscuits and gravy, bacon, and fried potatoes in the mornin. To fried chicken, mashed potatoes, and cole-slaw for supper. She also shared old family pictures and stories at each meal.

The first place Austin and Lane had to go after gettin there was Elvis Presley's birthplace. It was a two-room shotgun shack built by Elvis' father and uncle. For Austin and Lane, it was a chance to make a stronger connection to Elvis that would help them in their life. Austin was still in awe of the shotgun shack because it was so small next to Graceland in Memphis.

On Saturday evenin Larlee and Jean took Austin and Lane to Schlatter's diner for dinner. It gave Larlee a break from cookin, and they could all eat what they wanted to have. As they set down in a booth, they noticed all the commotion goin on in the corner booth at the south end of the diner. Breakin the silence as he looked at what was happenin Austin asked, "What's goin on down there?"

"Kelli King, Brittany Rhea, and Rosanna Aydelotte came in the diner to have a bite to eat." A tall slender dark-haired woman explained, as she got her order pad out of her apron.

"Rosanna Aydelotte is here?"

"Yes.."

Austin got up out of the booth, and started walkin over to where the girls were sittin. Lane set in booth watchin him with a big smile on her face as she shook her head havin and idea what would happen next.. Larlee and Jean were out of the loop and didn't really know what was goin on at all as they watched too.

Austin walked up as Rosanna signed the last autograph. After the young girl walked away from the booth, Austin stepped up to the table and asked, "May I get your autograph?"

"Of course." Rosanna said, as she took the napkin and started writin her name.

"Thank you."

"Who do I make this out to?"

"Austin Reid."

Rosanna looked up at Austin with the biggest grin on her face as she stood up, gave him a hug, and said, "Austin, why are you doin down here in Mississippi?"

"Hi, Rosanna."

Settin at the table Kelli King and Brittany Rhea looked Austin up and down. Kelli wasn't that impressed with him, but Brittany thought he was very cute. She thought that maybe she might take a swing at him and maybe have a summer fling with him. With a big smile on her face Brittany said, "Rosanna, who is this cute guy."

"This is my friend Austin Reid." Rosanna said, with a big smile. "He's the one that I spend Thanksgivin with last year."

"Wait, this is your Austin Reid. You didn't tell me that he was that damn cute."

Rosanna just looked at her with the funniest look and said, "Don't get any ideas he has a girlfriend back home. Don't you?"

"Yes, I do." Austin replied, crackin a grin.

"Too bad.." Brittany asked, as she made eyes at Austin.

"Wait, is this the Austin Reid that you've been writin to over the last couple of years?" Kelli asked, piecin together the puzzle.

"Yes, it is." Rosanna said, with a big smile on her face.

"Austin, it's nice to meet you." Kelli said, as she reached out her hand to shake his.

"It's so nice to meet you too." Austin said, as he reached out his hand and shook hers. "I'm a huge fan yours and Americana."

"So, what are you doin down here in this little Mississippi town?" Rosanna asked, as she looked over at Austin.

"My cousin has family down here." Austin explained, as he looked at all three of the women. "She's goin to have surgery in about month and we wanted to do somethin different then just stay in town all summer with the same borin things to do. What are you doin down here, Rosanna?"

"I just wanted to get out of New York for a while and just sort of relax before we start filmin again in the fall."

The four talked for a good hour and a half, and Austin got to know Kelli and Brittany a little better. After everyone had ate supper, Austin went back to Larlee's house and got his car. He followed Kelli back to her family's farm to visited witg them some more while Lane visited with her great aunt and cousin. Austin was impressed with the guesthouse Rosanna was stayin in on the property. He learned that they were slave quarters back in the eighteen hundreds when the King family was the biggest cotton farm in Mississippi. Kelli's mother had the quarters redone so when business associates came to the house but wanted their own space.

Around two o'clock the next mornin Austin was sound asleep with his head on the pillow when he felt a finger on his face movin around and a sweet voice say, "Austin, wake up..."

99

Austin opened his eyes turnin his head to see Rosanna lookin back at him with the biggest smile on her face as she kept pressin down on his nose. Crackin his boyish grin he asked, "Why?"

"I want to know what's behind those ice blue eyes, Austin."

"And this couldn't wait until later in the mornin?"

"No, I want to know what's behind them now."

Austin got up and looked at the clock and it was only two in the mornin. As he laid his head back down on the pillow he said, "I'm goin back to sleep we'll talk about it later."

Later that mornin Austin woke up around ten o' clock and walked out to the bedroom to the kitchen where he found Rosanna sittin atthe kitchen table readin the paper and drinkin a cup of coffee. As he poured himself a cup of coffee he asked, "Oh, what was you wanted to talk about?"

"What happened between us last night." Rosanna said, as she looked up at him from the paper.

"I know it shouldn't have happened because I am datin Jaelyn."

"But it did happen, Austin Reid. Now we need to figure out what we are goin to do so it either happens again or it doesn't."

"Sweetkins, I know that."

"What does that mean?"

"Elvis Presley's had nicknames for the special women in his life, so I decided to give you a nickname."

"You do have an Elvis Presley obsession, and is this one of the nicknames he had used in his life."

"Yes, I do have an obsession, and no this is a name I came up with myself."

"I guess, I'll have to come up with a nickname for you."

"Of course." Austin said, crackin his boyish smile as he took a sip of his coffee. "We need to try hard so that what happened last night doesn't happen again."

"Ok, we can try for not to happen again. But there are no guarantees that it won't happen again, King."

"Why are you callin me that?"

"It's my nickname for you." Rosanna said, crackin a smile as she took a sip of her coffee. 'I just came up with it."

A few days later Austin and Rosanna were at Schlatter's diner for supper. The two of them had cheeseburgers and french fries Austin started dippin his french fries into his shake before he ate it. Rosanna just looked at him a little dumbfounded because she had never seen anyone do that before.

"Is that good?" Rosanna asked, with a disgusted look on her face. "Why do you do that?"

"Lane and I started doin it when we were young, and we've been doin it ever since." Austin explained, as he took a bite of his fry.

"Ok."

"Why don't you try it."

"I don't know."

"Just one for me."

Rosanna looked at him with a funny look on her face as she picked up a french fry. She dipped into Austin's milkshake and held it in front of her before she took a bite of the french fry. After swallowin the bite that she took Rosanna said, "It is all right, but I wouldn't eat it every day."

Across the diner the Roccha family walked in, and headed to their normal booth. The Roccha family had a big cotton farm and Evan Roccha was fourth generation cotton farmer, and his wife Eva was in the high society of Saltillo/Tupelo. Eva was a drug counselor at the drug rehab center in Tupelo. She wanted to help people who were havin trouble helpin themselves. As the family walked by Austin's booth the two-year-old girl stopped and stared at Austin for quite a while. Austin noticed the little girl, she was a spunky chubby two-year-old with amber dark hair and captivatin blue green eyes, and said, "Hi, how are you?"

"I'm good." The little girl said, with a big smile. "I'm goin to marry you one day."

"Really?"

"Yes."

"What if he's married to me?" Rosanna asked, puttin her two cents into the conversation.

"I'm goin to steal him from you." The little girl said, very determined.

"You are? Why?"

"Yes ma'am, I'm goin to be with my sunshine, and he will want to be with me."

Austin went white as a ghost when the little girl said that, and he quickly walked out of the diner. Rosanna watched him a little confused wonderin what would make him run out of the buildin. She gave him a few minutes, and then she walked out of the diner to where Austin was sittin and asked, "Austin, what's wrong?"

As he looked up at her Austin replied, "I'm wonderin just howthat little girl knew my nickname because this is the first time I've met her."

"Maybe she heard one of the other women sayin your nickname." Rosanna said, as she sat down beside him on the sidewalk.

"The only person in this town that know that nickname is Lane, and she's not here. And the only person who called me sunshine was Jessica."

"Wait? So you believe that little girl is Jessica. The young girl that got taken away from you years ago."

"Yes.."

"I don't believe in reincarnation, and I think you are only hearin what you want to."

"I don't either, but Jessica told me that she would come back to me when I least expected it in many of the dreams I've had."

"They are only dreams."

"Maybe you're right." Austin said, as he wiped his eyes. "Maybe I am only hearin what I want to hear."

Across town Lane's uncle Virgil and Aunt Marlene were havin a catfish fry with all the fixins. All the family that lived in Saltillo was invited to come over.

"So how many surgeries will this be now?" asked Larlee, puttin a plate of food in front her

"Eight surgeries since I was three months old." Lane replied, with half a smile.

"You've been through a lot little one." Virgil said, huggin her. He was a plump baldin man who was always happy go lucky.

"Yes, I have."

"You may have been born up in Illinois," Marlene said, smilin. She was a tall plump woman with a heart of gold. "But you've got southern blood runnin through your veins."

"Yes, Ma'am!"

Everyone laughed because it was clear that Lane knew where she came from and was proud of it. The family enjoyed the visit since Lane usually came down once a year. After talkin about her up comin surgery, family members started tellin stories about her grandpa Sutton, and everyone called him Big Daddy.

Back across town Austin and Rosanna had walked back into the diner, and sat down in their booth. As they finished their food, Austin noticed the little girl watchin them with a big smile on her face. She would wave at Austin and he would have back. There seemed to be somethin about that little girl that seemed to want to draw Austin closer to her.

A few days later Austin and Rosanna went to Elvis Presley's Birthplace because Austin wanted Rosanna to learn everything about his idol. Rosanna knew of Elvis Presley, but didn't know about Elvis Presley. As the two went on the tour Rosanna found the history of Elvis very interestin, and couldn't believe that he was born in a shotgun shack with only two rooms. As they walked through the museum, both Austin and Rosanna couldn't get over the artifacts from the early years of Elvis' life. As they sat on the swing at shotgun shack Austin said, "Thank you for comin with me today."

"I had fun today and I learned so much." Rosanna said, crackin a smile.

"Hard to believe that the most recognized person in the world came from so little."

"I know."

Just as she said that a group of people walked up onto the porch and noticed who she was. One of the young teenage girls walked over to the swing and asked, "Are you Rosanna Aydelotte?"

"Yes, I am." Rosanna said, crackin a smile not wantin to deal with fans.

"Can I have your autograph?"

Rosanna took the pen from the girl, and signed the ticket she had to go through the birthplace. Then Rosanna took a picture with the girl and the girl's family. It wasn't long before more people started to come up to Rosanna askin pictures and autographs. Austin soon stepped up bein her bodyguard protectin her from all the people who wanted to get too close to her.

After gettin back to Saltillo Austin and Rosanna stopped at the diner to get supper before headin back to the King Farm. As they walked into Schlatter's diner that same little girl walked up to Austin and said, "You like drivin my car?"

"Excuse me?" Austin said, as he looked down at the two-year-old girl confused.

"You're drivin my ninety-six five ford mustang aren't you?"

"Why do you say that it's your car?"

"Because I had my daddy put green seats covers on it because it's my favorite color." The little girl said, very seriously. "My daddy gave it to you once he found the note I left in the glovebox. Not to mention the license plates have the name you called me since you were ten years old."

"I had to work on the car before my friend's father would give it to me." Austin explained, as he bent down to be face to face with the little girl. "And can you tell me what that nickname is?"

"There's a note in the glovebox for you, Sunshine. I wrote it not long after I got the car, so that if I was in the air force my father would give it to you once you got your license. And the nickname you called me was satnin."

Austin looked at the young girl and went white because he couldn't believe that little girl would know that. After regainin his composure Austin said, "Ok, I did call my girlfriend Jessica satnin since I was ten years old."

"Sunshine, I am your satnin, and you will find that letter in the glovebox." The little girl said, very seriously. "And I told you that I would come back to you when you least expected it."

"Ok. But, you have a wild imagination little one." Austin said, a little lost for words.

The little girl just looked at him with a familiar look that Austin knew very well because it was the look that Jessica had always given him when she was very annoyed at him. Then the young girl walked away to the table where her parents were at.

On Saturday night it was time for the weekly catfish fry at the diner, and many people in town came to Schlatter's for their weekly dose of catfish. Austin and Lane were hangin out with our group, and Beverly was tellin them about the band she and Christine wanted to start. She told them all about their family's legacy and how she and her cousin were goin to carry on that legacy when they got older. As Beverly was talkin a song came on the jukebox that made Austin look back to see who picked it to play, but there was no one around the jukebox at the time it started to play. The song was "The Moon Over Georgia."

"Cous, are you all right?" Lane asked, as she looked at him. She was a little worried because Austin had told her what had happenedat the diner with the little girl before.

"Yes, I'm all right." Austin said, scannin the diner to see who was in the buildin.

"I know this song is yours and Jessica's. Are you sure you're all right?"

"I'm all right." Austin said, as he got up out of the booth. "I justneed to go to the bathroom.

Lane watched as Austin didn't walk to the bathroom, but to the end booth on the other side of the diner. As he stood next to the booth he asked, "Do you like this song?"

"Yes, I do. In fact, daddy took me to the jukebox, and I picked it out myself. Did you check the car for the letter?"

"Really, no I haven't?" Austin replied, happy and confused at the same time. "What is your name? I forgot to ask."

"My name is Jessica Lynn Roccha."

"Really, and when is your birthday?"

"November twenty seventh."

"Really?" Austin said, startin to turn a little white after hearin answers. "Why do you like that song?"

"Because in my other life I loved the movie gone with the wind, and we watched it all the time." Jessica replied, as she stood up in the booth to look into Austin's blue eyes. "When the song came out in the spring of nineteen ninety-one you learned it on your guitar to play in the talent show at the Georgetown fair, and then we made it our song."

"I'm goin to have to set down." Austin said, as what she had said sunk into his spirit.

"Sir, are you all right?" Mrs. Roccha asked, as she saw the look on Austin's face.

"Yes, I think so."

"I told you I would come into your life when you least expected it, and you're scared that's why you haven't checked the car yet."

"Yes, I am. I've never had this happen to me before. Ok, if you are Jessica Roth, then where are your locket and promise ring that you wore every day?"

"Oh, I'm sorry to scare you." Jessica said, crackin a little grin with that look in her eyes that Austin knew very well. "I had taken them off that afternoon before I went for my bike ride."

"Why?" Austin asked, hopin to get an answer.

"Somethin told me I should, and I know now it is to give you a definitive sign that I'm back on the earth."

Settin across from them Jessica's parents were just lookin at her and Austin with funny expressions on their faces. It was all becomin clear to them now as they listened to their daughter talk to the young man because she had talked about her other life since she was thirteen months old along with learnin how to walk. And from six months old she loved to listen to Elvis Presley music.

"What about my dreams you're in, Satnin?" Austin said, as he looked into Jessica's eyes and saw the girl he was in love with before the tragedy happened.

"Yes, I love spendin time with you in your dreams. It just shows you that are bond hasn't been broken even though tragedy has happened. I know that you are overwhelmed by this, but when you get back to G'town go into my room look in my third dresser drawer under my favorite green sweater, and you will find my locket and ring. That I hope you will give back to me very soon."

"How could I have missed them. I've looked through your room in your house a thousand times since you were taken from me?"

"Sunshine, it's all right." Jessica said, as she started to play with his hair. "Your heart will be full of love and life again once you find out that I have come back to you again."

"It will be?"

"Yes, it will."

"What do we do in the meantime until you grow up?" Austin asked, as he looked at her wantin to know the answer.

"You live your life like we've talked about in your dreams."

"And what about Jaelyn?"

"Sunshine, Jaelyn is the girl who is supposed to be in your life right now."

"What about you?"

"I'm goin to be a kid and enjoy my life now." Jessica said, with a big smile and a laugh. "But you can write to me, and send me pictures of your life so I'll know what's goin on."

"Ok." Austin said, crackin his boyish grin. "And your parents can help you write letters to me until you're old enough, and send me pictures about what you're up to."

"Don't forget to add some of those pictures to our scrapbook, so that they will be in there when we get married to each other and add more to that book."

Austin looked at her and went white again because she had said somethin that shocked the hell out of him. He couldn't believe that she would know about the scrapbook, and it blew his mind just as much as everything else. Before gettin up from the table Austin got the Roccha's address so he could send letters to her.

An hour later Austin was comin out of the bathroom when he was met by Brittany Rhea. The awkwardness was broken when Brittany said, "You are so damn cute, Austin Reid. I could just eat you up with a spoon."

"Thank you, I guess.." Austin said, crackin his boyish grin.

As she pushed him up against the wall, Brittany gave him a very passionate kiss lettin him know that she was interested him. Austin didn't know what to think at first because he had never had a woman to do that to him before. Then bein a man he kissed Brittany back, but not with as much passion as she had put into the kiss. After the long kiss Brittany smiled and said, "If you ever break up with that girlfriend of yours call me. Here's my number."

Austin just looked at her as he wiped her lipstick off his lips. He just shook his head in amazement of what just happened to him. He looked down at the card that Brittany had given him, and sure enough her telephone number was on it. Austin laughed a little as he got out his wallet and put the card into it.

Bright and early the next mornin Austin and Rosanna were watchin the sun dance on the cecilin. Rosanna was runnin her fingers up and down Austin's belly as she listened to his heartbeat. As she ran his fingers through her long curly blonde hair Austin said, "If we are just friends why do we still end up in bed together?"

"You must secretly want me, King."

"You think so?"

"I'm startin to." Rosanna said, as she lifted her head up lookin at him.

"Would you like to go back to Illinois with Lane and I until you have to leave to start filmin again?" Austin said, as he lookin into her mesmerizin blue eyes.

"I would love to go to Illinois with you. To tell you the truth I'm kinda bored here doin nothin."

"Ok. I can take you around town and show you some of the spots that were important to Jessica and I."

"Will your girlfriend be happy that I'm there? I would love to get to know more about your relationship with Jessica. I'm also wantin to find out if what that little girl told you is true because it would change my mind on reincarnation."

"Probably not." Austin replied, as he cracked his boyish grin and laughed. "But I thought you didn't believe in that."

"After everything that she told you and the look on your face as you were tellin me." Rosanna explained. "I have to know because If it is true because it tells me that there is more to our bein than just livin and dyin."

Later that mornin around ten o' clock church started right on. Austin and Rosanna showed up just as Eloise, Christine, Lee Ann, and Beverly sang the mornin hymns. Rev. Schlatter walked up to the podium, started flippin his bible, and said, "I would like y'all to turn to Philippians 3:12. When you find it say amen."

People in the congregation begun openin their own bible turnin to the that book in it, and everyone soon begun yellin amen. "Paul says, not that I've already obtained all of this, or have I been made perfect, but I press on to take hold of that for which Christ Jesus took hold of me. Brothers, I do not consider myself yet to have hold of it but one thing I do; forgettin what is behind and strainin toward what is ahead. I press toward the goal to win the prize for which God has called me heavenward in Christ Jesus. We've got a hold of us even before we got saved. Still, we have to be hungry enough to search, and find out about our heavenly father. It takesdetermination to put the past behind you. We're not supposed to keep lookin back at the stupid things we've done. If we're plowin a field and lookin backward we'll never see our destiny in front of us. We need to keep lookin forward at the dreams and goals god has put in our hearts."

Rev. Schlatter talked for another twenty minutes before he finally said. "We all have a race to run in this life and we have a crown at the end of it. Like I said before it takes determination to finish the race. We do have to have a goal because if we just run with no reason will never reach the finish line. The goal we've got to have is to be like Jesus and to know our heavenly father. Let me end this service with a prayer. Dear Lord, thank you for sendin you son Jesus. I ask today that you fill the congregation with the spirit of determination to fulfill the plan you have for each of them. I ask this in Jesus name, amen and amen."

After the congregation said amen in agreement with Rev. Schlatter, the quietness was broken with chatter as people started catchin up with the local gossip. As Austin, Lane, and Rosanna said their goodbyes and walked out of the church, I sat there in the pew wonderin if I would ever see them again.

Order Form

Bell Sheep Publishing

214 E. 10th Street

Georgetown, Illinois 61846

(217)474-0410

Bonnie, Dexter & Jesus

Paperback book………………………$8.28

Small Town Dreams; Beginnings

Paperback…………………………….$8.28

Shipping

    1-10 books………………..$5.28

    10-20……………………….$9.28

    20 or more………………$15.28

Qty_____

Shipping_____

Subtotal_____

Total_____